Dear Reader,

I went to a friend's wedding recently, and was touched deeply by the ceremony, by the exchange of vows, by the circle of warmth encapsulating the bride and groom.

I felt how being near those totally and utterly in love has a lasting impact on all who share that moment.

I wanted to write about the women behind the scenes, the ones who make those special days happen, the ones who play fairy godmother, helping to create a memory built on love that extends beyond the span of days, months and years. The ones who, no matter how expert they are at helping others, can't quite sort out their own lives.

I hope you enjoy reading their stories as much as I enjoyed writing them. Look out for the third book in the trilogy, *A Convenient Groom*, #3809, coming next month in Harlequin Romance®!

Best wishes,

Darcy Maguire wanted to grow up to be a fairy, but her wings never grew, her magic never worked and her life was no fairy tale. But one thing she knew for certain was that she was going to find her soul mate and live happily ever after. Darcy found her dark and handsome hero on a blind date, married him a year later and found that love truly is the soul of creativity. With four children too young to play matchmaker for (yet!) Darcy satisfies the romantic in her by finding true love for her fictional characters. It was this passion for romance, and her ability to sit still every day, that led to the publication of her first novel, *Her Marriage Secret*. Darcy lives in Melbourne, Australia, and loves to read widely, sew and sneak off to the movies without the kids.

Books by Darcy Maguire

THE BEST MAN'S BABY

Darcy Maguire

THE WEDDING PLANNERS

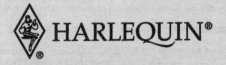

HARLEQUIN®

TORONTO • NEW YORK • LONDON
AMSTERDAM • PARIS • SYDNEY • HAMBURG
STOCKHOLM • ATHENS • TOKYO • MILAN • MADRID
PRAGUE • WARSAW • BUDAPEST • AUCKLAND

ISBN 0-373-03805-4

THE BEST MAN'S BABY

First North American Publication 2004.

CHAPTER ONE

MEN in tuxes. Yum.

Skye Andrews paused at the doorway of Camelot's bridal-wear boutique, breathing deep and slow, drinking in the sight.

Five men milled around the room, all tall, and all in superbly tailored black tuxes with white shirts and metallic-blue silk ties and handkerchiefs.

The men looked so clean, so proper and so absolutely charming, as though they'd stepped out of a fairytale and into reality. She wouldn't see a sight like this at a bar or a club.

She crossed her arms over her chest.

This end of the boutique was a great asset to the family business. Her younger sister Riana's flair for creating original gowns for today's brides certainly gave the business a great reputation and a crucial boost.

Today, however, Riana was nowhere in sight—she knew she wouldn't be needed with Camelot's resident tailor on the job and the boutique's sales assistants in action, handling the groom's party with ease.

Charlie knelt on the floor, pinning the hems on a very tall, very well-built man. Charlie glanced towards her, his thick moustache quivering as he plucked a pin from his padded wristband. 'What do you think, sweetie?'

5

Skye nibbled her bottom lip, trying to think professionally, but she couldn't help herself. She stood back and lazily perused the fine lines of Charlie's tailoring, and the man beneath the suit.

The black fabric sat on the man's square shoulders and swept down his arms, ending just before the cuff, making a striking contrast.

His hands were large. Skye closed her eyes—she could almost imagine the strength in them, roaming over her body. 'Very nice.'

She shook herself. It had obviously been too long since she'd had a man in her life. She straightened to her full height and smoothed back her hair where she had tied it at her nape. She had to get out more!

Charlie shuffled the pins. 'I hear you're taking over for your mum on this one.'

'That I am. Flu.' Skye looked around the men in the groom's party, wishing she wasn't coming into the wedding plans at the tail-end. She preferred knowing who everyone was and the hierarchy within the families before the plans got to this stage, and these were all the faces of strangers.

She dragged in a deep breath and lifted her chin. She'd just have to cope until her mother was back on board. 'Hello everyone.'

Most of the men in the room turned towards her.

'I'll be your new wedding planner until Barbara is back from the flu,' she said loudly, her cheeks heating at the awkwardness of the situation. 'Will the groom please step forward?'

The man having his trousers hemmed turned his

head slightly. 'What's the problem?' he asked in a deep, velvet-smooth voice.

Skye's chest tightened. That voice? It couldn't be. 'And you are?' she croaked.

Blood rushed through her ears. Not who she thought it was, and not the groom. Please, please, please, not the groom.

The man turned around.

Her heart lurched in her chest and thumped wildly, her vision blurring.

Nick!

It couldn't be. Not him, not here, not like this!

CHAPTER TWO

SKYE thought of the door, of running, but she couldn't tear her eyes away, let alone the rest of her.

His hair was still light, now a short-back-and-sides cut, but with the hair on top standing on end rather than combed back. His jaw was angular—she used to trail kisses down it, and his brow was creased—she *wanted* to step forward and smooth it with her fingertips like she'd done once, a long time ago, but she was frozen to the spot.

His deep blue eyes widened. 'Skye?'

'Nick,' she gasped.

'I am trying to pin here,' said Charlie from below.

'You look—' his gaze ran over her, over her simple grey skirt, white blouse and jacket '—wonderful.'

'You too.' She tore her attention from his brilliant blue eyes, looking directly at his chest, trying not to think about the man, in the flesh, finally being in front of her.

She opened her mouth but the words wouldn't come. What could she tell him anyway? Time had passed. It was way too late.

And he was getting married? She covered her mouth, trying to smother the wave of nausea racking her body. No. He couldn't be. Not after all she'd gone through, all the pain, the doubts and, ultimately, her sacrifice.

'What are you doing here?' he asked casually.

His deep voice washed over her like warm spring wind. 'I work here.' She swallowed, gripping the clipboard more tightly. 'I'm co-ordinating your wedding.'

'My wedding?' He lifted his eyebrows and laughed.

The sound rattled through her like a freight train. She glanced at the folder in front of her, the words a blur. Had she said something funny?

She shook her head. She was an idiot! Wouldn't she have noticed his name earlier if it were *his* wedding? 'You're not the groom,' she said tentatively, her mind still trying to grapple with his presence.

'Not a chance,' he said, his voice deep and smooth.

Skye let out the breath she was holding, feeling her knees shake under her weight. She took a tentative step, grabbing the back of the nearest chair. She looked at him. 'Then you are?'

'The best man.'

Skye stared at him. How did he know he was the best man for her? She shifted the weight on her heels. How could he know that he was the only man who had pushed her buttons? The only man who she thought of when she went to bed at night, the man who invaded her dreams and haunted her memories.

He crossed his arms over his formidable chest. 'I thought you worked in your family business?'

'I do.' She bit her bottom lip. 'I am.'

His blue eyes probed hers. 'You never said it was a wedding planning business.'

Skye swallowed hard. 'You weren't exactly looking favourably on the whole wedding scene.' She remembered his views on marriage and commitment intimately. If he'd known she was involved in the business he probably would have run screaming the first moment he met her.

Nick shook his head, his brow creasing. 'Isn't that strange? I never noticed that you didn't go into details about what you did.'

'You were too busy to notice,' she quipped. Her mind scrambled to make sense of meeting him again. He couldn't know, could he? The quick and disturbing thought welled in her throat. She swallowed hard. 'What are you doing here?'

His mouth quirked into a smile. 'I'm the best man, remember?'

She remembered all right. Every nerve in her entire body remembered him, mourned him, yearned nightly for him, measured every man that came through her life against him. 'Of course you are,' she said vaguely.

Nick smiled at her, his eyes glinting with purpose.

She shook her head. This couldn't be happening. She'd rehearsed it a million times. It wasn't meant to be here, like this. In a restaurant, in a club, or in a hotel foyer on some exotic trip she'd never taken, not here—she wasn't ready.

Skye dragged in a deep breath, trying to right her world again. 'I never expected you to be involved in all this—' she looked around at the suited men, at Nick and how well he filled out the tuxedo he wore '—how did you used to put it—*wedding stuff*?'

He shrugged. 'Times change.' And he let his gaze fall, skimming over her again, this time with a slow sensuality and an intimate thoroughness, as though he was remembering the magic they'd once shared.

Skye's belly tightened. She stepped backward, her cheeks heating. 'So, how are you?'

He smiled down at her. 'Good, and you?'

'Good.' Curiosity threatened to engulf her. There was no way she could ask him personal questions, not when four years lay between them like a chasm.

He looked good in a tux, and that blue silk tie set off the brilliant colour of his eyes. 'I hear you're with a prestigious law firm now,' she blurted. She bit her tongue. Dammit. Now he'd know she'd kept up with his career through the papers, the gossip columns and by whatever hearsay she could gather.

'Yes, I am,' he answered easily, his eyes narrowing. 'And you? Did you get what you always wanted?'

She just stared at him. What she always wanted…

She'd wished, dreamed and prayed night after night, day after day, from the day she had left him for what she really wanted, and now, here he was.

'O—kay.' She spun away from the man who'd stolen her heart and turned her life upside down. 'Is everyone happy with their outfits?'

There was a murmur of assent.

'Skye—' Nick's voice was deep and close.

'Right. Well, carry on then. I'm around if you have any questions,' she said to the men in general, ignoring Nick. She glanced at her folder, the words still refusing to be legible. 'Nice seeing you again, Nick… Mr Coburn.'

She forced herself to put one foot in front of the other.

'How about we have coffee later? Catch up a bit?' Nick was right behind her.

'I am trying to work here, folks,' Charlie whined, scuffling along the floor on his knees after Nick's trousers.

'No, I'm sorry. I can't.' Skye pushed through the doors, desperate to escape. The last thing she wanted to do was spend time with the man. She could hardly look at him for the wrenching ache in her chest, the sting behind her eyes and the torturous secret that stabbed her heart like a shard of glass.

He could never know.

Nick tore his gaze from the doorway.

He rolled his neck, massaging the muscles. It was only natural for him to react to her. She *was* even more beautiful than when they'd met four years ago. She was all woman now. And didn't he know it.

Her rich curves made his hands itch and just the thought of her full breasts, hidden beneath her white blouse, shot bolts of desire through his body.

Memories of trailing kisses over her smooth olive skin clawed at him, her deep red lips fired his blood and her sweet voice... Cripes, how had he ever let her go?

'Please sir, keep still.'

Nick stood motionless.

Her dark hair had grown. It was no longer a chic bob but long and sweeping, pulled back with wisps escaping and framing her gorgeous face.

Nick clenched his hands by his sides. He still had a thing for her!

Any wonder? Nick rubbed his jaw. She was the one that had got away.

At least she had the decency to look embarrassed about running into him. Cripes. After what she had done to him, it was amazing that she could look him in the face.

He hadn't seen a ring on her finger. Maybe the bastard that had stolen her away from him hadn't come up with the goods. Maybe he'd dumped her.

Nick smiled. That would be justice for all the months he'd tossed, sleepless, in his bed alone.

'Kindly stand still, sir.'

Nick looked down at the thin man hemming his trousers. He would have preferred one of the girls. He looked over to Pete who was chatting up the young blonde hemmer, and across to Tony, who was struggling to win a smile from the redhead.

Nick looked at the door. He'd prefer Skye at his feet, begging forgiveness…

He had really thought they'd had something magical.

Four years…it seemed like yesterday. They'd been clicking on all fronts. She'd understood his commitment to his career, could talk with him, and make his body wild in the bedroom. She was all he had ever wanted in a woman.

For six months they'd been together—it had felt like no time at all, as if he'd been cheated—then she was gone.

He hadn't realised she'd been seeing someone else.

He should have guessed. He had sort of felt that she had been slipping away in those last weeks. The more time they'd spent together talking about what he wanted in life the more she had seemed to distance herself from him.

He had thought it had been just a mood, or a phase. He clenched his fists by his sides. It had been another man.

He closed his eyes and took a deep breath. He never wanted to experience that sort of pain again.

He shrugged, trying to douse the fire deep in his body, trying to still his pounding heart and push the image of her wide, dark eyes from his mind. And the rest of her beautiful body.

He still had it bad. Cripes. Even after all these years...

He straightened tall and threw out his chest. He was older now, and a hell of a lot wiser. He knew what he wanted and what he didn't. And he didn't want to be haunted by Skye Andrews any more.

He was going to get that two-timing vixen out of his mind, body and heart, once and for all.

'All finished, sir,' the man at his feet stated dryly, getting to his feet and shooting him a far-from-pleased look. 'Finally.'

'Thank God.' Nick strode to the changing room, tearing the tie from his neck and flicking open the buttons on the jacket and the waistcoat.

Because he wasn't finished with Skye Andrews, not by a long shot.

CHAPTER THREE

SKYE gripped the phone tightly, her mouth dry. 'Tara, have you been in touch with Bridal Creations?'

'Not lately,' her older sister responded matter-of-factly.

'Weren't you going to snaffle one of their planners?' Skye crossed her fingers. Please say yes. Please let her say she has her. Please say she didn't have to put up with Nick Coburn in her face for the next couple of weeks.

She bit her lip, the reality seeping into her. As if a new girl could jump right into an ongoing wedding—she was delusional. She was stuck with the guy.

There was a tinge of hope for her—if the new planner teamed up with her and did the Harrison-Brown wedding with her then she could be Skye's assistant, and deal with the best man while Skye dealt with the bride and groom.

'I am thinking about it,' Tara said coolly. 'But there are several issues to consider when enticing an employee away. The main one being if she shows no loyalty to them, what chance is there that she'll show loyalty to us?'

'Money talks,' Skye blurted.

'And money invariably costs. More and more.' Tara paused as though she was considering. 'I'll have

15

to think of a way to entice her to work for us that goes beyond just a pay-packet.'

'Think faster.'

'Have you got a problem?'

Skye paused. She'd successfully kept the identity secret of the man who had changed her life years ago. Tara hadn't needed to know all the details then, and definitely not now.

Skye knew exactly what her sister would do and there was no way she wanted her bull-headed sister crashing into Nick and throwing accusations around and making demands...

She shivered. She didn't want a lecture from her sister either and Tara was damned good at those, having been in charge of the family's business for over three years.

Skye sighed. 'Just taking on Mum's wedding client on top of—'

'I've got everything else under control, Skye. I have two weddings of my own on the go, as you know, but Maggie and I will take care of all the bookings and follow-ups with everyone but the clients themselves.'

Skye sagged back in her chair. 'But you don't know—'

'You've documented your progress well.'

'I have?' She sat a little taller. Praise from her older sister was rare, but then, having a man like Patrick in her life made a big difference. It was amazing what a little love could do.

'So don't panic. I spoke to Mum just an hour ago. She has every confidence that the Harrison-Brown wedding will go off without a hitch if she's not back on board before the fateful day,' Tara stated dryly. 'Oh, and she sounds terrible so please don't hassle her unless absolutely necessary.'

'Sure.' Skye stiffened. There was no way on earth she could talk to her mother about this. She was worse than Tara when it came to being bull-headed. 'I don't foresee any problems.'

'Good.'

Skye rang off. No problems. Except that the man she'd walked out on four years earlier was back in her life!

Breathe. Just breathe. There was no reason to panic. *She* would hardly see the guy, probably didn't need to see him at all. She nibbled her lower lip. She could probably avoid the man completely until the rehearsal and the wedding.

She strode to the window and stared out at the busy street. Was one of the cars outside his? Had he gone yet? Had he had his fitting done, taken off that amazing tux, and gone back to his life? She crossed her fingers and leant her head against the cool glass.

Did he have someone in his life? She bit her bottom lip, a chill sweeping through her.

She stared out at the sky. Nick probably didn't even think twice about running into her. Odds were it had to happen eventually. She just wished it was still years down the track, when she was older, more mature, stronger and far more capable to cope with surviving an ex-boyfriend who was a lawyer.

Skye sighed. Nick had probably already dismissed her from his mind as an old girlfriend, over and done, and that was all she was. He had enough of those running around the city, from what the papers reported.

She licked her dry lips. It was probably a daily occurrence for him. There was no reason to think there was anything more to it.

She heard the knock and the door open. 'Just put the cup on my desk, Maggie.' She needed the cuppa desperately, but she wasn't about to show Maggie that, or the fact that she was bothered.

'I would,' said a distinctively male voice. 'But I don't have the cup and I'm not Maggie.'

Skye swung to face him, her insides coiled tight. Nick!

Nick Coburn wore a dark suit that silhouetted his shoulders as nicely as the tuxedo had. His white shirt and deep green tie were neat, pressed and tidy. Did he have someone ironing his shirts for him? She stiffened. Or was he just sending them out? 'What are you doing here?'

A smile tugged at the corners of his mouth. 'I told you, I'm the best man.'

She took a deep breath. Where was her professionalism? Where was her detachment, and all that cool, calm sense that she'd employed in her life so well over the last few years?

'What can I help you with?' she asked as calmly as she could, avoiding looking at the man directly, trying to slow the thunderous pounding of her heart and the flood of heat to her face.

'I'd like to discuss my speech at the reception. I need some advice.' He strode across her small office and dropped into the white fabric sofa in the corner as though he was perfectly at ease.

She lifted her chin. 'Oh, of course.' Professional she could handle. She just couldn't afford to go anywhere near personal, or go into details of what exactly *had* happened four years ago.

'Shoot.'

He scrutinized her, his gaze intense, as though he was looking into her very soul...

A shiver raced down Skye's back, sending ripples of awareness across her skin and into her body. She crossed her arms over her chest and concentrated on breathing and not on the barrage of questions tossing around in her head.

Nick arranged several of the red heart-shaped cushions around him and then gazed directly at her. 'I'm not sure whether I should go with a joke to start my speech with, or not?'

The tension in her eased a little. Work mode, she could do. 'There is a popular misconception that the best man has to be witty, funny and entertaining.' Skye strode behind her wide white marble-topped desk, sitting down in her red chair, pretending this was just any other man in her office. 'Be funny if funny works for you. But it's more important to be genuine.'

'So your advice is—?'

She arranged some papers in front of her, concentrating on what she usually said to the best man and not on the rush of blood in her ears. 'Keep it simple, genuine and brief.'

'Okay.' Nick clapped his hands together and

rubbed the palms against each other, not taking his eyes off her. 'Understood.'

Skye stood up, the hairs on the back of her neck standing on end. 'Is that all?'

Nick didn't move. He looked at her, the intensity in his deep blue eyes disconcerting. 'Don't you want to hear it?'

'What?' She bit her bottom lip. Why he'd come? Why he'd shown up in her life now after all these years or what he'd heard somewhere, what he suspected? Her heart pounded against her ribs. Or what he wanted now?

'My speech.' He leant his elbows on his knees, his blue eyes gleaming. 'Do you want to hear it?'

Her knees gave out beneath her and she sagged back into her chair. 'Sure.' She waved him on. 'Sure, go ahead. I'm all ears.'

He rubbed his hands together. 'Terrific, but it's not quite ready at the moment so I'll be back when the first draft is done.'

'Great.' She sighed. She should have seen that one coming. 'Not a problem.'

He leant forward, his eyes probing hers. 'Are you sure? You seem a bit tense.'

Skye lifted her chin. 'I assure you, Mr Coburn, that no matter what went on with us in the past I am a professional. I'll do my job where the Harrison-Brown wedding is concerned. No problem at all.'

He shot her a curt nod. 'You don't have a problem with me being the best man?'

'Of course not.' She was obviously transparent. She pulled back her shoulders and met his deep blue eyes.

'It was four long years ago, Mr Coburn. It has no relevance here today.'

A muscle quivered in his jaw. 'I'm interested in finding out how your life has gone during those *long* years, Skye.'

Her name on his lips sent a shiver down her spine. She raised an eyebrow. 'I don't see that it's any of your business.'

'I'd like to make it my business. We were friends once,' he said, his voice low and smooth. 'Don't you owe me at least a cup of hot chocolate?'

Her chest tightened. He'd remembered her favourite drink! She shook her head vehemently. 'I don't think so. Besides, we didn't part on the best of terms.' She'd made sure of that. She couldn't have him looking her up a few months down the track. She'd had to make it final.

'Really? I hardly recall.' He stood up and smoothed down his trousers. 'But it's just a cuppa. Unless your husband wouldn't like it?'

'I'm not married,' she blurted, heat rushing to her cheeks.

A smile teased the corners of his mouth. 'So, there's no argument then. Say, twelve o'clock at that café down on the corner.' He cocked a thumb in the general direction.

Skye opened her mouth but no words would come. He was as arrogant and as confident as she'd suspected from his reported exploits. Which only made him more dangerous than ever.

She wanted to slap herself in the head. She should have left that question about a husband unanswered.

It would have been better for her if he thought she was committed to someone. She would have been safe. 'I—'

He shut the door firmly behind him.

She closed her mouth and stared at the door. Nick Coburn wanted to meet her later, wanted to talk, wanted to catch up on old times, and catch up on what she'd been doing these few years?

She covered her mouth, stifling the urge to scream. If only he knew!

What on earth was she going to do?

Nick Coburn tapped the melamine table-top with his pen, staring through the café's front window for the hundredth time. He glanced at his watch—it was past twelve-thirty.

Maybe he should have waited for an answer from the woman, but dammit, she sent his mind and his body into a spin just being near her.

She *should* come. If only driven by curiosity.

Skye had always been punctual, considerate and giving, except for having a damned affair under his nose. He ran a hand through his hair. He wouldn't have thought she'd be the sort of woman to juggle two men, play the field to that extent. It had baffled him for years. His sweet, innocent girlfriend had turned out to be a stranger.

Another lesson notched up. And she was a hard lesson.

He stared at the papers in front of him blankly. It would probably be best if he kept his current *modus operandi* and stayed the hell away from her. Dating models was great for his image, his ego and his exposure to the general public. Just not so good for his sanity or his wallet. Luckily he kept each affair brief. He glanced at the door to the café. But it was time for a change.

His mobile shrilled. He grabbed it and stabbed the button, his body already warming at the thought of her. Was she running late, stuck in traffic somewhere or going to offer an apology? 'Coburn.'

'Nick, how'd you go with your fitting?' Sandra's voice was sweet and lilting.

He looked at the ceiling. Sandra was tall, blonde and wily. Almost model material. He'd met her several times at Paul's place and then at the engagement party. She probably would have made for a nice distraction but now, after seeing Skye again, feeling what she stirred deep inside him, he had bigger challenges at hand. Like getting her out of his system once and for all.

'Mine went fabulously. That designer that Camelot has there is amazing. You should see our bridesmaid dresses. They're unbelievable. No sleeves, no straps, just cupping my breasts and then sweeping down. All soft, pink and silky, caressing my skin like you wouldn't believe.'

'Really?'

'Oh, yes. And you should see what she's done with the wedding gown. Goodness, that's the only place to get your dress. It's all white with off the shoulder straps that are extensions of the dress rather than just straps. And all studded with tiny pearls and the finest lace around the edges. Then there's the veil… But silly me, rattling on like this.' She paused for breath. 'How did *you* go?'

'Fine.' He looked towards the door.

'I bet you looked so amazing in your tux. I can't wait for the wedding, can you?'

He didn't want to hear about himself. He didn't want to hear about her dress, or the wedding. He looked at the door, his body tense. He wanted to know about Skye. 'What do you know about the planner and the business?'

'Darling, I know heaps, of course. I wasn't going to let Cynthia just take on any wedding planner. Camelot's going to do Kasey Steel's wedding, you know? It's in early spring. It's been splashed through all the papers.'

'What about the planners?'

'Well, they're all sisters, three of them, and then there's the mother. The oldest sister does a bit of wedding planning and proposal planning. What will they come up with next?'

'I don't know.' He twisted his cup, watching the remains swirl around the bottom. 'And—'

'And then the youngest is the fashion designer. She does all the dresses and they are to die for.'

'And—'

'And the mother and the middle daughter are the main wedding planners. It's so cute, isn't it? Keeping it in the family.'

'Very cute. What about details?'

She dragged in a deep breath. 'Well, I know they shot out of mediocrity with the announcement of their doing the Steel wedding. Before that I don't think they were as motivated or something. I don't know. But I know the wedding planner daughter was not even there full-time.'

Nick straightened the depositions in front of him. 'What else about the young wedding planner woman? Do you know anything else about her?'

'Why do you ask?' asked Sandra, her tone sharp and biting.

Nick clenched his hands. 'No reason. Just that the mother has come down with the flu, apparently, and the young one is taking over Cynthia and Paul's wedding.'

'Really? Well, I hope she's good,' Sandra stated dryly. 'And I hope she's decided to take her job seriously and do it properly.'

'Sure to.' It was obvious Sandra's knowledge didn't go far. No surprises there. 'Look, Sandra. I have to get going. Work and all.'

'Of course. Sure.' There was a long pause. 'Well, bye then.'

Nick hung up and stared at the mobile. What else could Skye possibly have been doing if she wasn't working at Camelot full-time? A course at university? Another job? Another man?

He gulped down the last of his coffee, almost cold, swallowing hard. He pushed the unpleasant thought from his mind. First things first.

He plunged the phone back into his jacket pocket and looked at his watch. Almost one. His lunch hour was up. He gathered the papers in front of him—he'd hardly looked at them. He had to get over Skye as quickly as humanly possible and get back to focusing on his work.

He stood abruptly, almost skittling his chair. Skye was surrounded by unanswered questions and he had every intention of getting all the answers, by whatever means possible.

Whether he liked the answers or not.

CHAPTER FOUR

'SKYE, you have a phone call on line one from John, line two from the Macdonalds, and line three from the Donovans—a new query.'

Skye smoothed back the wisps of hair that had escaped her *coiffure* and sighed deeply. The phone had been ringing half the morning and most of the afternoon since she'd run into Nick. If she'd had to cope with bookings and follow-ups to caterers, florists, churches, reception centres and all the rest as well, she'd have gone mad.

'Tell John I'll call him back later.' Skye was glad she was too busy for *that* call. She'd have to explain why she had left a message on his answering machine cancelling their date. 'The way things are going, much later. Ask the Macdonalds if *you* can help them. Tell them I'll ring them back otherwise. I'll take the new query.'

'Okay,' Maggie chimed.

Skye punched the phone for line three. She looked at her watch again. Almost five. Only a few more minutes and things would slow down. She could finish the day's work and run home.

She needed to take a hot shower, scream into her pillow and sort out what on earth she was going to do about Nick Coburn.

She answered the Donovans' queries easily. She'd

done this enough times to know all the answers to all the questions couples came up with when they wanted to hire a wedding planner. She wished her life were as easy.

'Skye, I'm heading home. Anything else you need me to do for you before I go?' Maggie swung her head around the door.

'No, I'm fine. Just itching to get home.'

'Yeah, it must be really weird for you to be here so late.' Maggie hooked her bag over her shoulder, wiping her nose with a tissue. 'You're usually gone by two.'

'Can't be helped. With Mum sick—' She looked at the work still in front of her, her stomach leaden. She hated being this late home.

'We should send her flowers.'

Skye nodded. 'She'd like that. Remind me tomorrow, can you?'

'Sure. Night, Skye.'

'Night, Maggie.' She was a great asset and an enthusiastic young woman who was eager to help with all aspects of the business.

The work was tedious. She felt every minute passing like a deep thud in her chest. If only Tara could dig up another planner from somewhere to lighten the load, she could get back to the routine that worked best for her.

At six she couldn't take it any more. She tidied her desk, grabbed her coat and purse and flicked off the light. The rest could wait until morning. She had responsibilities that were more important than work.

Skye moved through the darkened offices. The qui-

etness of the place at night was almost surreal after
the hectic bustle of the day.

She rarely got to hear the silence. Not for years.
She had her hands totally and utterly full at home.

She poked her head around the door of Tara's office and smiled. Empty. There were days when
Maggie swore Tara spent the entire night working.
These days, with the new guy in her life, her sister
was lucky to get *in* to work on time.

She flicked off the last light and let herself out,
locking the door securely behind her. She sighed. She
hadn't locked up in years either. So much had
changed in her life...

'You didn't show up.'

Skye swung around, her heart leaping in her chest.

Nick stood behind her, looming like a brick wall,
dark suit, dark coat and a very dark look.

'I know,' she managed breathlessly.

He came close, looking down into her face, his jaw
set firm. 'Would you like to give me an explanation?'

'Would you mind if I caught my breath? You startled me.' She touched her chest, trying to still the
pounding of her heart. It was just the scare. Nothing
else. 'This isn't the day and age to be jumping out at
women late at night.'

'You have nothing to be frightened of from me.'
His voice lowered dangerously.

She doubted that! She swung away from him and
strode towards the car park, thankful that the street-
lights were all intact. It was a good neighbourhood—
she just didn't like taking chances.

His footsteps were heavy behind her.

'Really? Nothing to be frightened of from you?' she tossed over her shoulder. 'I can't imagine that you've grown up that much.'

'You'd be surprised.'

She darted him a quick glance. Surprised at how little he'd grown? Sure, he'd filled out some more and his face looked a little less fresh, but he was the same Nick Coburn she'd known. She was sure of it.

'I'm fine to get to my car on my own,' she snapped, lifting her chin and lengthening her stride.

He came up beside her. 'I'm sorry if I gave you the impression that I drove all the way out here to escort you to the car park. I'm here for answers.'

Skye faltered. Did he know? She shook her head, urging her legs to walk straight to her Mitsubishi sedan. She pressed the auto entry pad, watching the light inside go on, illuminating the back seat.

Damn. She froze, her cheeks heating and her pulse raging through her body. Damn, damn, damn.

Nick caught her arm and turned her to face him. 'Skye?'

She looked up into his strong face, his jaw sporting a slight shadow, his hair mussed a little as though he'd been working on a difficult case.

'Okay. Okay.' Skye stared at his chest. 'If you'd waited around for me to respond to your invitation in the first place you would have discovered that I'm flat out.'

'You were working?'

'Yes. Working. Flat out busy and couldn't spare a minute—disasters...you know.' Skye looked at the ground, where his shoes met the pavement, unable to look into his face on the off-chance that he'd see the lie in her eyes.

'You could have called,' he stated casually.

She looked up at him. 'Where? I know nothing about you.'

Nick stood in front of her, boldly intimidating, the soft light from the street-lights casting shadows across his face. 'You know I work at Stevens and King. You could have called there.'

She bit her lip. Caught out. Damn. She'd thought about it but figured he'd talk her around in circles until he eventually got his own way. 'I didn't think—'

'Hmm. Yes.' Nick's voice was cutting. 'I can see that as a bit of a trait of yours.'

She crossed her arms over her chest, glaring up at him, eye to eye, a swell of indignation surging up her body. 'What is?'

'Not thinking of other people.'

Her blood heated. 'You know nothing about me. My entire life is thinking of other people. Twenty-four seven.' He had a nerve. She baby-sat people's weddings, co-ordinating hundreds of people, a myriad of details, all for other people. And then there was home, where she barely got two minutes to herself...

'Tell me about it,' he said softly. 'All about it. I want to know.'

She shook her head, clamping her mouth closed. She'd fallen into that one. He had a way of getting people to say things and there was no way she could afford to fall into that trap.

'I'm interested,' he said softly, slipping his hands into his trouser pockets.

Skye shook her head. 'You're just interested because I was the one person in your life who decided not to play your game.' She put her hands on her hips. 'I said no.'

'Other people have said no to me.'

'And gone unscathed?'

He laughed. 'Not exactly.'

A hot ache fired in the pit of her stomach at the deep rumble of his laugh. She lifted her chin and glared at him. 'Leave me out of your games, Nick,' she snapped, fighting her body's traitorous response.

Anger. Her only strength was in anger. She couldn't afford to weaken. She shrugged out of her suit jacket and opened the back door, tossing it across the back seat. She couldn't afford for him to see what was in the back. She jerked backwards and slammed the door.

'They aren't games, Skye,' he murmured, reducing the distance between them, looking down into her eyes, at her lips. 'I'm all grown up now.'

She stepped back, swallowing the ache in her throat and resisting the urge to moisten her lips and look at his mouth. Memories coursed through her mind and body, of the magic his lips could evoke in her, of what they'd once shared, of how much she'd lost.

She pressed her legs against the cold steel of the car, grounding herself. 'That only means you're more dangerous than ever.'

'Thank you.' He looked down at her, his face half-shadowed. 'But I promise I won't bite. Come to dinner with me.'

'I'm sorry, I can't.' She looked at her watch and cringed. 'I have to get home.'

'Another man?'

She shook her head. The accusation, and his tone, took her back four years. He hadn't taken her leaving him well—she'd had no choice but to agree to his assumption. Rejecting him totally and utterly on every level had been the only way to ensure that he wouldn't come after her. 'It's none of your business.'

'I'm trying to make it my business,' he said softly, his voice deep and velvet-edged.

'Please don't.'

'You're telling me that you're not married, not in a serious relationship, yet you're refusing me?' He crossed his arms over his chest. 'On what grounds?'

'Sanity.'

'Ha!'

'Go back to your tall, lanky models, Nick. Leave me out of it.' Skye grabbed the door handle.

He raised an eyebrow. 'So, you're intimidated by what you've read in the papers?'

She paused. Darn. She hadn't meant for him to know how closely she'd been following his life. 'I'm hardly a model, Nick, and you have to admit they have been your standard fare of late.'

'Agreed, but that's not because of their looks,' Nick said carefully, running his gaze over her as though he was cataloguing just how different she was from his blonde bombshells. Maybe that was the point.

She stared down at the door handle. 'But they make good trophies hanging off your arm.' She nearly had enough clippings of him with one pretty woman or another to fill her shoebox—almost as though he was trying to outdo himself, or set a record.

He stiffened. 'Well, yes, they do, but it's more that there's a mutual understanding that the relationships are superficial.'

She let go of the door handle and turned and faced him, crossing her arms over her chest. 'Do you tell *them* that?'

He shrugged. 'Not in so many words.'

'I wouldn't think any woman would like to think she meant so little to you.' She rubbed her arms, her body chilling. Had she meant so little to him? 'You're a chauvinistic ass, you know that?'

'In my defence, I make sure every woman that comes into my life knows how little I think of commitment and marriage and all that junk.'

'And if she had any argument?' She knew from experience how clever he was at arguing his point. It was all she could do to keep track of the original dispute and her stance when she'd locked horns with him on one issue or another.

'You didn't.'

Skye shook her head. 'I was young and foolish.'

'You were beautiful. *Are* beautiful,' he said softly.

'Save your sweet talk for someone who cares.'

'You don't?' He raised his eyebrows, his eyes wide and deep, almost giving him a touch of vulnerability. 'You don't think very highly of me, do you?'

She shook her head, not trusting herself to say anything to that. What could she say? He'd been her world…

'We were good together, Skye.' Nick's voice was deep and husky. 'Remember?'

She swallowed the lump in her throat and shrugged. 'But some things aren't meant to be,' she said as calmly as she could. She opened the car door and slipped inside.

He put a hand on the car roof and leant over her. 'Some things could be worth another shot.'

She froze, her heart skipping a beat, looking up into his eyes, their brilliant blue colour shining in the light from the car. 'What are you saying?'

He shrugged. 'Come out to dinner with me.'

She shook her head. She was dreaming. Her wish could never come true. Nick Coburn was driven by his career—nothing else mattered. 'I told you, I can't.'

'Tomorrow night, then?'

She shook her head, fighting every nerve in her body and every dream in her silly head. There was no future with Nick Coburn.

He pulled back, straightening tall. 'I'm not going to give up on you easily.'

'Then I'll make it hard.' Skye slammed the door of her car and shoved the key in the ignition. She twisted it and the engine roared to life.

She flicked on the headlights and pulled out of the car park, vividly aware of the dark form standing rigid, watching her.

She had too much to lose to make anything easy for Nick, way too much. And she knew him too well to let him anywhere near her defences, because when she was with him, she didn't have any.

Nick was a disaster waiting to happen.

CHAPTER FIVE

SKYE pushed open the front door to Camelot, her mind a jumble of clients, times and Nick.

She looked down at her watch. She was late this morning, but she'd had to make up for coming home so late last night.

She hoped her mother would recover quickly so she didn't have to keep working to this extent, especially anywhere near Nick.

She froze in the doorway. The foyer was filled with flowers—yellow roses, red roses, pink roses, white roses, carnations, daffodils and bunches of mixed blooms, all vibrant with colour. She breathed in the sweet scent, as if she'd stepped into a flower shop or a much-loved garden on a warm spring day. 'What's all this?'

Riana stuck her head out from behind a grove of carnations. 'It's what it looks like—a lot of flowers,' she said, a cheeky grin across her face.

'Nice to see you.' Her younger sister was an amazing designer, specialising in wedding gowns, with an artistic temperament and a total disregard for office hours. She flitted in and out as she pleased, doing her gowns, and that was about all.

Riana picked up a rose and put it to her nose. 'And nice to see you. Mum being sick must be a bummer for you.'

Skye nodded. 'Rick's being romantic with Tara again, is he?' Skye's chest filled with a beautiful warmth as she looked around the foyer. She was so glad her sister had found someone to love, and someone who loved her so much. It made her think that happy-ever-afters weren't so impossible after all.

She pressed her lips tightly together, fighting the sting behind her eyes. Tara was so lucky.

Skye pulled one of the closest yellow roses towards her and dragged in the warm, rich scent. It was her favourite flower. She remembered all the times that Nick had brought home yellow roses for her.

He'd been an amazing lover. Romantic and caring—in the hours they had together, just brief snatches in time. The rest was work. All work. His driving need to be all he could be his primary focus.

She'd accepted that, and loved that passion for his work in him. She was busy too, and it was only later, when life had thrown her a curve-ball, that she had discovered there would be no future for her with Nick Coburn.

'No.' Riana rearranged the flowers in one of the bouquets. 'The flowers are not for Tara.'

'You?' Skye could imagine her younger sister having a string of boyfriends willing to make such a grand gesture for her. She was pretty, young and full of energy.

Riana smiled. 'They're for you.'

'Me?' Skye's breath caught in her throat, her heart pounding against her chest. She stepped forward tentatively, touching the small card that lay nestled in the nearest bunch.

Say Yes.

Nick! She'd thought yesterday that he was bluffing. Today... She looked around her and cringed. He had to have bought the entire florist's stock!

She bit her bottom lip. She knew what he was like with challenges in his life—tenacious, stubborn and devious, not to mention dogged. She'd seen him go after cases, seen his determined study at night, seen how his mind worked.

She was in trouble!

'So, are you going to say yes to the mystery guy? It isn't John, is it?'

She shook her head. John. She hadn't thought of him at all. She slapped her forehead. 'I forgot to call him back.' He was the latest in a series of dates set up by her mother, okay company but nothing like Nick.

'I didn't think so. John doesn't strike me as the romantic type and especially not the type to splurge a heap of his hard-earned money on this—' Riana drew in a deep breath '—amazingly romantic gesture.'

Skye wished he had. John would have been easier to handle than Nick Coburn, and she suspected that romance wasn't exactly what Nick had on his mind...

'So what should I tell him?' Riana looked at her expectantly, brushing her dark hair off her face, looking as much like a manic matchmaker as their mother.

'Nothing.'

Riana raised a perfectly arched eyebrow at her.

'Where's Maggie?' She was usually in at this time

of day. And, of all people, Riana would know—the two of them hung out together a lot of the time.

'She called in to say she felt sick.' Riana perched herself on the small corner of the reception desk that didn't have flowers on it. 'She figured a day of rest, chicken soup and watching a soap or three would fix her up. And I decided that I could man her desk for her while I design the Macdonald gown, and Tara's, too.'

'That's great. Thanks.' Skye bit her lip. The last thing they needed was Maggie out sick for any length of time.

'So—' Riana clapped her hands and grinned. '*Who* should I tell that answer to?'

Skye stiffened. 'Nothing to no one.'

'No reply? To this? Are you crazy?'

A delivery man strode into the room with flowers in his arms. 'Another delivery for Skye Andrews,' he stated dryly. He placed the three foot high bouquet of red roses, complete with glass vase, on the floor beside Maggie's desk.

Riana stared at the vase then at Skye. 'We'll drown in flowers if you don't answer him.'

'Okay, we'll answer him.' Skye looked around the offices, willing her mind to work. 'Where's the shredder?

'You're not going to shred all these beautiful flowers? You can't,' Riana squeaked. 'Skye?'

Skye strode across the reception area and froze in her office doorway. If she'd thought there were a lot of flowers in the foyer there were twice as many in her office. Every surface was covered in them.

'Riana!' She turned back to her sister.

Riana strolled up to her, standing beside her in the doorway. She shrugged. 'The first delivery guy was here waiting when I opened up this morning.'

Skye stared at the beautiful bouquets. Just how many deliveries had there been? 'How am I going to work?'

'Say yes.'

She shook her head. The fact that every flower was one of her favourites and there weren't any that she disliked meant something. Did Nick keep notes in his little black book on each woman he dated—how else could he have remembered?

Skye strode across her office to her desk. If he thought that she was still the young girl she'd been when he'd first met her, he was mistaken. She'd grown up. She wasn't going to roll over and accept anything at face value, especially this.

She knew what he was like, knew what games he liked to amuse himself with, knew how much he enjoyed getting people to roll over on their previous decisions and come round to his way of thinking.

He wasn't going to get that sort of satisfaction from her, not after everything she'd been through.

If Nick Coburn wanted to play, fine. She had a few games of her own!

Nick flicked another page in the deposition, glancing at the phone again. Any minute now and she'd call him and say yes. He couldn't help but smile.

Her place would look like the Botanical Gardens by now. He couldn't help but smile. If she had been in any doubt that he was serious about his invitation to her, she wouldn't be now.

He looked at the clock on the wall. Hell, she was stubborn. She'd lasted longer than he'd first thought she would. How many flowers did a girl need to conclude he was seriously interested in taking her out?

Nick would do whatever it took. Money was not an issue. He felt a swell of satisfaction. Just to think it made him taste his sweet success. He'd done what his father, and his brother, hadn't.

Marrying his mother at twenty-two had, as far as his father was concerned, put paid to his aspirations of becoming a lawyer. He said it had doused his energy and his drive, sucking away his commitment to going back to school.

Nick knew his father had struggled to make enough for their family to get by, sometimes doing two shifts at the factory.

Six children was a bit much. With all the bills, clothing and then feeding them all, his parents barely managed most of the time.

Nick Coburn didn't want that for himself. No way. And neither did his father. He wanted his sons to achieve what he hadn't.

He toyed with the pens on his desk. He'd seen his father put all his energy behind his older brother, Robert, encouraging him through school, cheering him on in his achievements at university and urging him to greater career aspirations.

Nick had seen his father shake his head at his brother's lack of drive. Heard his criticisms of him when Robert had got all serious over a woman. And seen him cry at Robert's wedding.

Nick had never seen his father cry. It hadn't felt good. It had felt like a giant hammer had slammed the air out of his lungs.

He didn't want to feel like that again. Ever. He was going to get where *he* was going—come hell or high water. Nothing was going to stop *him*.

He'd make his father's dream come true for at least one of his sons before he left this world.

A knock sounded. His office door opened and his secretary came in quietly, carrying a steaming cup of coffee. She hovered next to his desk.

He could smell the heady brew. 'Thanks, Liz.' He took the cup from the greying woman. 'Any news?'

Liz pushed her glasses up the bridge of her nose. 'I just heard that there's been a spate of anonymous deliveries of flowers to hospitals, to nursing homes, and to medical clinics all over the city.'

Nick coughed, splattering coffee over the desk.

'Oh, dear.' She rushed out of the door and was back again, her hands full of tissues and a box of them under her arm. She mopped up the coffee.

Nick pulled a handful of tissues from the box and dabbed the documents in front of him, trying to clear his throat.

'Are you all right?' she asked.

'Fine.' He hadn't expected that! He fought a smile. Skye was something else. There wasn't an atom in his body that doubted that the flowers were his.

Liz walked to the door. 'Some people have money to burn.'

'Yes, well. Thanks, Liz.' He tossed the clump of sodden tissues into his bin. 'But I was actually referring to what you may have heard around the office about the promotion.'

'Oh. Nothing yet, sir. They say they're going to meet early next week to discuss who'll make senior partner.'

'Okay.'

She turned at the door, her face creasing as her smile widened. 'It was a lovely gesture, don't you think? The flowers. It would have put a lot of smiles on a lot of faces.'

'Yes.' Nick rubbed his jaw. Skye would be smiling all right. The vixen. She was meant to be ringing him with her 'yes', thanking him profusely for his incredibly romantic gesture of sending so many flowers to her, not playing philanthropist.

He stared at the work in front of him—it could wait a few minutes. What was *her* problem? It was only dinner…

He wrenched open his top drawer, pulling out his address book. She wanted to play hard to get? Wanted to torture him some more with what he couldn't have?

He flicked the book to the right page. Only this time he wasn't prepared to walk away.

He punched the numbers on the phone. But first, he needed all the facts.

CHAPTER SIX

'I HAVE good news and maybe not so good news.'

Skye looked up from the prices she'd got from the caterers for the Macdonald wedding. She had hoped to get more than a few minutes work in before anyone realised she was back from lunch. 'Riana?'

Riana smiled, swinging her arms wide. 'The good news is the flowers have stopped coming…and the design for Tara's gown is going to be the best one yet. I've made the bodice form-fitting, strapless, with the most gorgeous cut around her cleavage—she has very nicely shaped breasts, you know. And over the fabric on her breasts I'm putting the finest pearl lace and, flowing down around her ribs, beaded drops that look like delicate icicles, so she looks like she's a ballerina princess, only with a long, flowing gown. And I'm putting pearl beads on some of the panels on the gown too and—'

'Riana!' Skye looked up from the file on her desk. Her office was back to the way it had been, except for the one large bouquet of yellow roses she'd kept, for old time's sake.

'Okay. I'll stop rambling. But isn't it fabulous that the flowers have stopped?'

She nodded slowly. 'Great.'

'You don't sound thrilled.'

Skye forced a smile. 'I'm surprised they stopped so soon.' It wasn't like Nick to concede defeat.

Riana shrugged. 'I heard about all our donations on the radio when I was out to lunch, so I guess he did too.'

Skye shook her head. 'He'd be too busy to listen to the radio…but someone he knows may have.' She chewed her bottom lip. 'Pity. I'm sure there were plenty more places where people needed cheering up that we could have sent flowers. I guess our days as Robin Hood are over.'

'Well…' Riana rummaged through Skye's pencil holder, avoiding looking at her. 'Mum liked those chrysanthemums we sent on to her.'

Skye nodded. She would have given her week's wages to see the look on Nick's face when he heard what she'd done with them. The bill from their regular delivery guy to send them on would probably be the value of her wages this week, but it'd be worth it.

Tara would have a fit, but at least Nick wouldn't see her as a pushover now. She grinned. She wasn't young any more, not about to go all weak-kneed and starry-eyed over him and his grand romantic gestures. Not this time.

'The not so good news— I think…' Her sister faltered. 'Is…well, come and see for yourself.' She gestured over her shoulder.

Skye watched Riana dawdle to the door, looking over her shoulder at her with a strange look on her face. It wasn't like Riana to be coy or backward.

She stood up and moved around the desk, wary. What could possibly have caught her sister's tongue?

Skye forced her legs to move to the door. She hadn't seen the foyer since this morning—she hadn't wanted to see all those flowers again—and had used the back way to go to lunch. The last thing she wanted was to contemplate the enormity of his gesture, or what it really meant.

The foyer looked so much bigger without all those flowers—Riana had left a couple of displays of red roses, placed aesthetically around the foyer.

The ribbons caught her eye first. Then the boxes— gold boxes, bronze boxes, silver boxes piled up on Maggie's desk and beside it. 'What?'

'They're chocolates.' Riana looked at her cautiously, as though she were a ticking bomb. 'I know how much you like chocolate, and it will take a lot longer for the room to fill up than with the flowers...'

'I don't believe it.' Skye sagged against the doorjamb, overcome with Nick's enthusiasm. She knew getting rid of his unwelcome attention couldn't have been as easy as distributing his gifts around the city.

'There are...a few more.' Riana pointed to their mother's office, biting the end of her pencil and glancing at Skye warily.

Skye strode to her mother's large office and froze in the doorway. Every surface was covered in chocolates. Boxes of chocolates, baskets of chocolates, bowls of chocolates and great platters covered in ornate handmade chocolates.

'I'm so sorry. I didn't mean for it to get quite so out of hand. You were out so I told the delivery guy to stick his delivery in here.' She put her hands on her hips. 'Then I went to the bathroom and when I came back… He must have had a truckload!'

'It's okay. That's okay.' Skye stared at the display. What did he think he was trying to achieve? Did he think she'd weaken on her decision just because he'd sent her a few thousand dollars worth of flowers and half a ton of chocolate? He was mistaken.

She shook her head. One box of chocolates and one bunch of flowers represented a romantic gesture, represented a sweet encouragement to go out with him. This much—she stared at the sheer extravagance of it—was overkill.

Skye straightened tall, lifting her chin. What was he trying to do? Flaunt his wealth, or his determination? Or just blackmail her into going out with him with the threat of drowning her in gifts of one sort or another?

She lifted her chin. She'd learnt a lot the last couple of years, especially to fight for what she believed in. And there was no way she would let a guy blackmail her into going out with him just because he was out to hamper her business with his gifts.

Riana leant against the door-jamb. 'I'm sorry. I didn't think anything of it and you were on your lunch break— Okay, I got caught up in my drawings and didn't take any notice of the delivery guys… *I* like chocolate.' She shrugged. 'Hell, what girl doesn't? But I didn't really expect a repeat of before.'

'How'd he have time for this?' Skye whispered, more to herself than to her sister. The man was a junior partner already, and darned successful at that. He had to be too busy for all this…hadn't he?

'You're kidding, right?' Riana shot Skye a look of consternation. 'These days a phone call will get you anything, including a chocolate shop. And then there's the internet where a click here and there and *voilà*, you have a ton of chokkies at your door. Or ours.'

Skye sucked in a deep breath. She was right. And they smelt so good. He knew the way to a girl's heart, but this much was the way to the nearest weight clinic. 'Okay. We can handle this like we handled the flowers.'

Riana fidgeted in the doorway. 'We could. I'm sure we could. But what happens if he sends something else?'

Skye shook her head. She was right. Nick Coburn would probably start sending her whatever else he thought was romantic, *in excess*.

Riana smiled wickedly. 'I can see it now. Baby rabbits, chicks, kittens or puppies…?'

Skye jerked her chin up. 'Right. You're right. Can you send whatever else that comes over to the offices of Stevens and King?'

Skye glanced back into the office. 'And don't worry about these. Mum won't be back at work this week and, besides, it wouldn't hurt to keep a few.' She managed a smile. 'I like chocolate. You like chocolate. Do your friends?'

Riana grinned. 'And who do I tell the delivery guys to send them on to?'

'Nick.' She swallowed hard, her chest tight. 'Nicolas Coburn.'

'Oh, my goodness.' Riana clapped her hands over her mouth and smothered a whoop. 'The best man in the Harrison-Brown wedding?'

Skye ignored her. 'The best pain in the butt,' she qualified. 'How do you know him? You haven't been helping Charlie with the tailoring again, have you?'

Riana was known to 'help' Charlie, just to check out the prospects in the wedding parties.

'No. But I did pass through when Charlie was measuring them all up for their suits and I have to say, sis, that that Nicolas Coburn has *really* nice measurements.'

Skye bit her bottom lip. She should have known.

'Why wouldn't you want to go out with *him*?' Riana tilted her head to one side. 'He's tall, blond and gorgeous.' Riana wrapped her arms around herself and smiled, her eyes bright.

Skye's heart contracted. 'We have a history.' It was a relief to finally share the fact. She'd kept it bottled up inside for so long.

'He isn't—?'

Skye shook her head vigorously, her cheeks heating. That girl was quick! Too quick!

Riana pointed her finger at her and waved it like she was scolding her. 'Oh! He so is. I can see it now. I'm such an idiot. I knew the guy looked familiar somehow. My God, does he want to make up?'

Skye clamped her mouth shut. What could she say? She didn't know what he wanted and she was terrified to find out.

'He does know, right?' Riana caught her gaze. 'You have told him, haven't you?'

Skye shrugged and shook her head, moving closer to a large basket of chocolates, covered with red cellophane and topped with a red bow.

'What are you doing?' Riana crossed her arms over her chest. 'It's been years. He should know.'

'He's a lawyer,' Skye said softly, peeling back the cellophane and breathing in the rich scent of the dark chocolates.

'Oh.' Riana wrapped her arm around Skye's shoulder. 'Oh, hell. Do you think he knows? What are you going to do?'

Skye shook her head. She had no idea. 'He doesn't seem to take no for an answer.'

Riana glanced around the office, her gaze moving from one stack of chocolates to the next. 'No, he doesn't seem to.'

Skye picked up the biggest, roundest, richest looking piece of chocolate and put it in her mouth, savouring the flavour of one of the few creature comforts she afforded herself.

She blinked several times, trying to dispel the sting behind her eyes. Had he remembered how much she loved chocolate?

'Is he a good lawyer?' Riana asked tentatively.

Skye swallowed hard. 'Yes, why?'

'Just because in all the movies, you know, the lawyers stick investigators on the people that are being difficult, turning their pasts over and inside out. So they have ammo against them.'

Skye coughed hard, almost choking. Riana was

right. That would be just what Nick Coburn would do if someone was getting in the way of his goal, and for some insane, reason his goal was to get her out on a date with him. And, by the looks of all this...and the flowers too, maybe more than just a date.

Her heart pounded wildly against her ribs. There was only one thing for her to do. She dragged in a deep breath, praying to the heavens.

She only hoped she could pull it off.

CHAPTER SEVEN

NICK loosened the knot on his tie, throwing his case on the sofa and kicking off his shoes. What a day.

He had three cases going concurrently. Two civil actions and a custody case. He was up to his eyeballs in depositions, research and reports. And, despite it all, he couldn't stop thinking about Skye.

Nick had thought initially it was because she was being so stubborn, enticing him to think about more ways to romance her into his way of thinking. But she'd called. Accepted his invitation. And he was more distracted than ever.

After this date, he'd be over her. He'd get all his questions answered and prove to himself that his curiosity was the only reason he couldn't stop thinking about her. That the unanswered questions were what was behind her haunting him.

His apartment was too quiet. He shrugged off his suit jacket and threw it across the back of the sofa. And cold, despite the polished timber floors, the soft lemon walls and the bold colours of the furniture that his sister had chosen to decorate the place for him.

The large open-plan space with multi-level living was usually just perfect, but even the floor-to-ceiling windows didn't seem to help today. The dull grey of the city sky just perpetuated his mood.

He flicked the buttons on his shirt. Maybe he

should get a dog. He'd like a dog eagerly waiting for him to come home. But having a dog in an apartment wasn't ideal.

Although it was a top of the market unit, and architecturally designed, its economic use of space didn't allow for a large dog. And he'd want a big one, like the Labrador that had turned up half-starved at his back door when he was a kid.

He'd loved that mutt. Fed him, walked with him and played with him for that whole afternoon. But he couldn't keep it. It had been enough for his parents to feed all the kids and pay the rent, let alone a dog as well.

It didn't help that his father had been a heavy smoker, using what little extra they did have on his habit.

Nick yanked the shirt out of his trousers. He'd have to get a house, with a yard out the back like the one he'd bought his parents two years back. One with a yard big enough for a large dog to run and play in.

Nick climbed the narrow staircase and strode along the small balcony overhanging the lounge to his bedroom and swung the wardrobe doors wide.

A house in the suburbs wouldn't be totally intolerable. Driving a bit further to work wouldn't be a big hassle compared to having a bit of space around him. Even his father would have to see that having a dog wasn't like getting burdened with a wife and children and everything else it entailed.

He'd had this place long enough. Sixteen months in April. He'd keep it and use the equity to buy the house, just in case suburbia didn't agree with him.

It wasn't as if he was going to settle down or anything. Oh, no. His father would keel over and die on the spot if he saw another son throw his dreams away for the house in the suburbs with a picket fence and a wife.

He pulled out a black suit and a shirt. Nick had grown up listening to his father's stories of men that he'd known in school going on to make amazing careers for themselves. They were mostly for Robert's benefit, being the oldest, but he'd listened too, with rapt attention.

The wistful tone with which he had recounted the tales had seeped into Nick like water into the roots of a tree. He was determined to make the old man proud, more so since Robert had opted out, giving up on meeting the old man's expectations.

Hell, there was no way Nick was going to make the same mistakes that his father had drilled into him to avoid, as a child, as a teen and every time he saw him. He wasn't about to disappoint him, especially now.

He couldn't exactly see how having someone to share your life with was *that* bad. He could see that having children could slow your career if you took the time to enjoy them. And hell, who wouldn't want to, if you had them?

The time would come, but not now.

For now, there was nothing wrong with playing the field, looking for affection wherever he could find it. There were plenty of warm women willing to share cold nights with him. And plenty that didn't mind a no-commitment relationship.

Was Skye at that point in her life?

Nick stripped off the rest of his clothes and strode into the bathroom. He was itching to find out what had happened to the jerk that she'd left him for. What had gone on? And gone wrong? She obviously wasn't with him now or she'd have a ring on her finger.

He turned the taps on, throwing back his shoulders. She'd said yes to his invitation to dinner—that had to count for something. He couldn't help but smile.

He was close now. Close to clearing up all his questions so he could get on with his life. Free from her haunting face, her harsh words echoing through his dreams, and the confounding question as to why she had preferred the other guy to him.

Life would be normal. He could go out with whoever he wanted without his mind whispering Skye's name. He could kiss a woman, be with a woman, without thoughts of Skye drifting into his mind.

He'd finally be rid of her, and his life would be perfect.

Skye sat nervously at the bar, tapping the counter with her nails. She'd come extra early to ensure that Nick wouldn't get it into his head to come anywhere near her house.

She nodded to the barman for a refill. One tropical cocktail wasn't enough to face Nick Coburn. There possibly wasn't enough alcohol that she could consume that could allay the deep rumbling of danger through her mind and body.

Had he stood her up? She closed her eyes and prayed he had. Maybe all he was after was a bit of revenge for what she'd done to him yesterday, leaving him waiting at some café, though it wasn't likely that he'd sat around for her for more than ten minutes.

She swished her drink. She could live with being stood up. It was better than considering what would happen if he did come—question after question. Lie after lie.

So, Nick Coburn had got his way by getting her to agree to go out with him but she was going to get hers. So, Nick Coburn wanted to rekindle the memories of the past that she tried daily to forget. She was going to talk him in circles.

'Sorry, I'm late.'

Nick's velvet-smooth voice washed over her. She turned on her stool, her gaze running over the black suit he wore, tailored perfectly around his large frame. His shirt was a soft blue silk, the top buttons undone, revealing a light scatter of hair on his chest.

He was as devastating to her senses dressed casually as he had been in that tux. Her blood heated and her heart pounded against her ribs in an oddly disconcerting rhythm that stirred her entire body from the tip of her toes to the top of her head, every nerve on alert.

Skye bit the inner lining of her mouth, trying to quell the stirring deep in her body. She was crazy to be here.

'Traffic was wild.' Nick signalled the barman. 'Scotch on the rocks.'

'Nick—'

'Have you been here long?' He smiled down at her,

his eyes bright and his mouth curving sensually. 'Wow, that dress is…amazing.'

She cast her eyes to his black shoes, her cheeks heating. He didn't mean it. Not really. It was just customary for a man to compliment his date—he meant nothing by it.

She chided herself for her reaction to such a clichéd statement, however deep his voice was, however his gaze moved over her.

She forced a smile to her lips. She'd tortured herself for long enough about what to wear. She didn't want to look drab and plain just in case he figured himself lucky on his escape. Or too fancy, just in case he got ideas that she couldn't possibly entertain. She decided on being safely, simply stylish.

The soft cream dress was elegant, with small thin straps holding up the light material, the bust line low, revealing the soft swell of the top of her breasts, the fabric form-fitting, hugging her ribs and stomach, all the way down to her thighs, where the dress flowed to just below her knees.

'Would you like to go eat?' he asked, his voice husky.

Skye nodded. Yes, she wanted to eat and run. She wanted to get this over with as quickly as possible with minimal disruption to her sanity, and her life.

Nick Coburn had wanted a date. Fine. She was here. She'd do this and she'd be fine—cool, calm and controlled. She wasn't a love-struck girl any more, willing to be romanced, willing to fall in love and give her heart away. She was a woman, with more responsibilities than he could imagine.

Skye slipped off her stool, striding ahead of Nick, eager to outdistance him. She didn't want his gentle touch at her elbow guiding her—she wanted to avoid his touch altogether.

The room was magnificent. Chandeliers almost the size of small cars hung from the high ceilings that were as ornate as the door trims—all carved in intricate detail in the image of flowing vines and flowers.

Royal purple tablecloths covered the round tables dotted around the room, with two ornately carved timber chairs at each. A pianist was playing in the far corner of the room, the sweet melody evoking an intimate sense of romance.

'You like?' Nick asked.

'I love.' She surveyed the sheer size of the room. 'I wonder if they do receptions?'

'For weddings,' he said flatly.

'Yes.' She swallowed. It probably wasn't a bad thing to remind him of what she did for a living, just in case he fell into the delusion she was just another one of his conquests.

'You should ask, later.' He pulled out her chair for her at the table the *maître d'* had gestured to in the corner of the room.

Always the gentleman. Her chest tightened. She'd loved that about him when they'd first met, as though he'd read a book on chivalry and was all for making it an art form.

She stepped to the chair, staring directly ahead of her, holding herself still. He was too close to be glancing at him, smelt too good to get any closer to him or his soft lips and deep blue eyes.

She chewed her bottom lip. She was so confused.

She dropped on to the chair, her legs as tired as her mind. His knuckles grazed the bare skin on her back and a shiver raced down her spine, just like the old days.

The *maître d'* flicked out her napkin and laid it across her lap.

The stupid urge to grab the man and beg him to join them was excruciating. She wasn't ready to spend time alone with Nick Coburn. Not really, no matter what she told herself. 'Thank you,' she offered tightly.

The man nodded, barely breaking his sombre expression, and handed a menu to each of them. He bowed low, and inched backwards.

'I'm so glad you said yes,'

Skye took a breath. 'I'm so glad you stopped inundating my office with deliveries.'

'You didn't like them?' He sounded surprised.

'I love flowers and I love chocolates, but everything in moderation.' She managed to smile. 'What were you going to send next, the seven plagues of Egypt?'

He looked at her, his blue eyes intense. 'No. I would have come begging on my knees.'

She raised her eyebrows. 'Right. I can't see that ever happening.'

'Okay. Maybe you're right.' He grinned. 'You know me pretty well.'

She nodded, rearranging the cutlery in front of her. How could she not? They'd been together for almost six months. She'd known everything about him, intimately.

The waiter arrived at the table. 'Are you ready to order?'

Skye registered Nick's glance at the untouched menu that still lay closed in front of him. 'Sure,' she blurted before he could respond.

She flicked the menu open. The quicker this night was over the better. She scanned the list. 'For entrée I'll have the quail,' she blurted. 'For the main—' she nibbled her bottom lip, skimming the list '—the chicken in orange sauce with roast vegetables. And for dessert…the chocolate mousse.'

Nick cast her a glance, his eyes narrowed. 'Your prawn entrée please, a steak medium well done, and the mango cheesecake,' he stated, his gaze steady on her.

'And the wine, sir?'

'I'll have a glass of your house red with my main.' He picked up his scotch and took a sip.

'I'll have the white.' Skye shifted in her seat. He was the same Nick she'd known. Not to be outdone in anything, even in something as ordinary as ordering a meal at the drop of a hat.

'You're efficient,' he murmured.

She straightened the napkin on her lap. Did he see through her? Did he know she was trying to get this over with? 'Just hungry.'

He nodded, putting his drink down slowly, his blue eyes unsettlingly intense.

'Why were you so committed to—' she swung her arms wide '—this?' Nick was never one to do anything without good cause, and she hoped she could handle it, whatever it was.

'I want to hear about what you've been doing.' He swirled his drink, the ice clunking against the glass. 'So, tell me. I'm all ears.'

She shrugged. 'Nothing you'd be interested in hearing about.' She held her hands together tightly on her lap. 'Nothing terribly exciting.'

'Right. Okay.' Nick didn't sound convinced. He took another sip of his drink. 'Well, what happened to that fellow that you left me for?'

She plucked up her drink and took a gulp, finding it hard to swallow. 'There's…nothing to tell.'

Nick leant forward, resting his elbows on the table. 'What *was* his name?'

'I don't think I said.' She looked towards the doors to the kitchen, praying for food to come so she could shove it in her mouth and feign a polite silence.

'Well, tell me now.'

'You want a name?'

'Yes.'

'John,' Skye blurted. Curse her stupid tongue. Why she gave Nick the name of the man she was currently dating she had no idea—desperation, or self-destruction?

'What's his occupation?'

She fiddled with her napkin. 'He's an accountant.'

'And it's over?'

'Ye—es,' she said tentatively.

'Is he tall? Short? What?'

She took a sip of her drink, lingering over it, stalling for more time. 'I don't think that's any of your business.'

'It was certainly my business when you left me high and dry for the man.'

'Nick—'

'You owe me this much at least. Surely. I've thought about the man a bit. Speculated a great deal on this matter. I'd appreciate your assistance to put it to rest, okay?'

'He's been on your mind?' She chewed her bottom lip. If her fictitious John was on his mind, then was she also on his mind? Did he have regrets?

'He's been like a pebble in my shoe.' He sat taller, throwing out his chest. 'Like a quandary that needs an answer.'

She swallowed. It was for his ego's sake, then. Typical. 'Okay.' She'd tell him whatever he needed to know, and she knew from experience that lies worked best if they were based on truth. 'John's tall-ish, not quite as tall as you. He's got dark hair, he's kind and charming and has…hazel eyes.' It wasn't like Nick would meet up with John, so it wasn't a problem, and keeping to the truth would ensure that there was far less chance of being caught out in her lies.

Nick's mouth tightened. 'Did it last long?'

She tightened the grip on her glass. 'What?'

'Your relationship with the guy that you left me for…did it last long?' he asked tightly.

She shrugged. 'A while.'

'And then—'

'Then, I've been busy with work.' Skye picked up

her drink and took a sip, hoping she looked far calmer than she felt.

'Too busy to socialize?'

She shrugged. Busy? She hadn't known the word until she'd tried to juggle her new life with her career.

'You're not giving me a lot here.'

She crossed her fingers on her lap and prayed that she wasn't about to be struck down. 'The last four years has flown by. Not much to tell, really.'

She'd decided years ago on her course of action. He'd made abundantly clear his need to succeed, his need to achieve things his father couldn't and his brother wouldn't. She'd seen his dream burning in his eyes...and had known that if she really loved him she'd let him go.

It was as much the case today, if not more so—he had even more to lose. He was so close to having everything he wanted, and she was the last thing in the world he'd want turning up in his life now, especially with the added extras she now carried with her.

The entrée arrived. Skye feigned starvation, despite the protests coming from her stomach as she forced the delicacy down. She could hardly think, let alone eat, since Nick had come back into her life.

She was uncomfortably aware of Nick watching her as she tackled her quail. What he was thinking she had no idea. Turmoil raged in her body. Did he by any chance know the truth and was just playing with her? She wouldn't put it past him. 'How are your parents?' she blurted.

'Fine. My older brother, Robert, has had his third child.'

'Congratulations.'

'Yes. Well...' He took another swig of his Scotch.

'Oh, that's right. It's condolences. The bane of life, kids, eh?' Her stomach tightened.

He shrugged. 'I guess it's good. After all, it doesn't really make a difference after the first child. What's done is done. And, I have to admit, they're pretty cute.'

She held on to the flare of heat, resisting the urge to pick up something and whack him on the head. She skinned the last bit of flesh from the quail and chewed slowly, holding her knife and fork tightly in her hands. 'You see Robert much?'

Nick shrugged. 'Not as much as I'd like. Too busy.'

Skye nodded, placing her utensils on the plate. 'And your sisters?'

'They're good,' he said warmly, his attention on the waiter removing the dishes. 'Tanya is in marketing. Lisa has gone into interior decorating, Kylie is doing arts in university and Rachel is in her last year at high school.'

Skye tried to smile. She'd really liked his sisters—she would have loved to have seen them again to see how they'd turned out. She pushed the wisps of hair escaping from the coil at her nape. But that was impossible. It was all impossible.

The waiter arrived with the main meal, the plates laden with a colourful array of vegetables and wafting sweet luscious scents in her direction.

Skye concentrated on putting one forkful of food into her mouth after the other. The chicken was melt-in-your-mouth sweet and tangy from the orange sauce and succulent, moist, and filling.

Skye only wished she could enjoy the meal without the heavy weight in her chest. Any minute now and he'd spring the real reason for this date on her.

Did he know?

Nick put down his knife and fork, resting the backs of the implements on the tablecloth. 'The reason you left me was because you loved this other guy, right?'

Skye choked on her chicken. This was it. He'd discovered the truth and was going to tear her quiet little existence to pieces.

She coughed, covering her mouth with her napkin. This was it. The moment she'd dreaded for the last four years, all her nightmares rolled into one.

After this, life would never be the same again.

CHAPTER EIGHT

SKYE finally raised her head, looking him directly in his deep blue eyes, her heart thundering in her chest.

She took a gulp of water from her other glass. 'Of course I loved him,' she said with all the calm she could muster. 'He meant the world to me.'

She bit her lip, staring down at the contents of her glass, praying. If he knew it was all a lie there was no point in any of this—he was playing with her. If he didn't—she couldn't afford for him to guess that she was lying through her teeth.

A muscle in Nick's jaw clenched. 'You really loved him?'

'Absolutely, truly, really, with all my heart and soul,' she enthused. If she was going to go down, she may as well go down flaming.

His grip tightened on his glass. 'Well, obviously not absolutely or you would have stayed with the guy.' His voice was thick. 'What happened?'

She gulped some wine, hoping to push down the lump of food in her throat. She stared at what was left of her meal, wondering how she'd manage it. 'He left me.'

'Left *you*?' He sounded incredulous. 'Why would anyone want to leave you?'

She glanced at him, her mind scrambling for an answer for him. 'Another...another woman.'

'No.' He shook his head. 'Not a chance.'

Her stomach lurched. He knew! 'Nick I—'

'He couldn't have been in his right mind,' Nick bit out, raking her with his gaze, his blue eyes burning.

Skye stared at him, her chest tight, every breath she took burning her throat. He was either going to lay his cards on the table or he was out to sweet-talk her into his bed.

She twisted her hands in her lap, her body fluttering in excitement and dread.

'You flatter me,' she said slowly, concentrating on her meal, pushing the vegetables on the side around with her fork. 'But yes, we were together…six months before he—' She paused, her mind struggling for a plausible tale.

'You should have called me,' he said softly.

She looked at him, shaking her head. 'No, I couldn't have.'

'You would have been upset. I could have been there for you.' His tone was gentle, his jaw set. 'I could've been your rock.' He shrugged. 'I hear my sisters talking about rocks, shoulders to cry on and men.'

She couldn't help but smile. 'That's sweet of you, but I couldn't have.' She probed his blue eyes. She couldn't imagine going to Nick after breaking up with him for someone else. Couldn't imagine him just sitting by and listening to her story, had it been true.

Was this all a ploy? A game? A trick? She took another mouthful of vegetables, trying to stay calm and alert.

He picked up his implements and stabbed his steak,

grinding his knife through the meat. 'Tell me about the wedding planning business.'

She looked up at him. 'Really?'

'Sure. I'm interested.'

Skye breathed a sigh of relief. *He didn't know.* Thank the heavens. Her quiet little existence was safe from Nick Coburn.

She lost herself in the rest of the meal, in his kind interest and his warm eyes. She spoke carefully, mindful of what she said, savouring the rich flavour of her dessert and Nick's riveting blue eyes.

She was safe. Nick didn't want anything more from her than to catch up on old times, just like normal people did when they ran into each other after years apart. Not a problem.

Skye moved restlessly in her seat, looking towards the doorway. If that was all he wanted, then why on earth had he gone to such an extreme to get her here? All those flowers and chocolates had to mean something.

Nick picked up his credit card from the dish the waiter had left and stood up. 'Ready?'

'Sure.'

He touched her arm lightly, steering her out of the crowded restaurant, the heat from his hand branding her flesh and searing her blood, the heat racing through her body.

Skye looked around at the other couples, their chairs together, their heads bent close in conversation, their eyes shining brightly for each other. Her chest ached. She missed that.

Maybe she'd set her standard too tall, blond and

hunky. Maybe there *was* someone else out there for her, just waiting for her to take the time to find him. Maybe...

Nick pushed open the front doors and they stepped out into the cool night air. Skye wrapped her arms around herself, rubbing her skin, trying to ward off the chill in Sydney's autumn air.

A body-warm jacket dropped over her shoulders. 'May I have the honour of taking you home?' Nick asked, his voice deep, velvet-smooth and close. Too close.

Her heart skittered. Was he asking her to share the night with him? Her body heated, her blood racing through her veins.

All the nights she'd gone to bed dreaming just that, remembering his hands running over her body, making magic, his lips taking hers.

She shook her head, trying not to breathe in the scent of Nick on the jacket—cologne mingled with the intoxicating hint of pure Nick Coburn.

'No,' she gulped. 'I'm fine. A taxi is fine.'

'Are you sure?'

'Absolutely. I've had a nice evening and you've been good company,' she blurted. 'I'm glad we've talked and cleared the air.'

'So am I.' Nick moved around to face her, looking down into her face as though he wanted to finish the evening the way they always had.

Goosebumps erupted on her skin and her body ached in places she'd rather have forgotten.

Skye dragged in a ragged breath. 'So, I guess I'll see you at the rehearsal dinner for the Harrison-

Brown wedding.' And then the wedding, and hopefully that would be the end of this chapter in her life. 'Goodbye, Nick.'

Nick pushed his hands into his trouser pockets. 'So, that's it?'

She nodded. That was it. Obligation met, air cleared and questions answered. They could go their separate ways and she wouldn't have to see Nick again.

Her throat closed up, her chest aching. Over.

Nick stared down into her face, his eyes shadowed as though he was battling an internal war. He pulled his hands out of his pockets. 'What the hell.' Nick pulled her into his arms, his mouth capturing hers.

Skye put up her hands against his chest, set to push him away, but his mouth was hot, and hard, and felt so nice.

His lips plied hers with a gentle mastery that warmed her from head to toe, his mouth strong and familiar. Images jumped to her mind from the past, of making love on the rug on the floor, in the back seat of his car, on the kitchen benches, and on the smooth, clean sheets of the bed they'd shared for almost six months.

Skye languished in the sensations rocking her mind and body, in the memories of a time when her life was simple and uncomplicated, when to love a man was to be with him, sharing his life, when having him was all she had ever wanted, that and a family of her own.

It was so good to touch him again, taste him, be with him…she could have stayed in his arms for ever.

She slipped her arms around his waist, holding on to him, just for a few beautiful minutes…

His arms were around her, enveloping her, pressing her close against his solid body, holding her safe, steady, warm.

She knew better than to trust what she was feeling. This was just a kiss goodbye. That was all. She relaxed into him, opening her mouth to his sweet exploration.

Nick didn't hesitate, deepening the kiss.

Her senses went wild, her blood firing as desire slid, hot and fiery, through her. She ran her hands up his back and returned his kiss, her lips burning with the passion of fourteen hundred lonely nights.

He felt so good.

It was like it used to be…although he wasn't hers any more. He was into models now—tall and lanky, with as little commitment to a lasting relationship as he had.

Skye pulled back, breathing hard.

She could do this, and she could walk away, knowing that this was the end of it, their last kiss…

Nick knew it. She knew it. All her naïve fantasies were over. They could never be. She'd been a fool to think it could be any other way.

She sucked in a deep breath of cool air, trying to still her thundering heart and cool her blood.

'Goodbye, Nick,' she blurted. She swung away from him, forcing her legs into action.

She couldn't look back, couldn't falter, couldn't let him see how much she still loved him. And she loved him to the very core of her being, but it could never be.

He was the same man that she had left four years ago. Nothing had changed—he still wanted his career more than he wanted anything else in his life.

There wasn't going to be a happy-ever-after for her like in fairytales. There wasn't room for her in her his life, no matter what he made her feel.

CHAPTER NINE

NICK watched the taxi drive away, the red tail-lights like a beacon. He wanted to go after her. Kiss her again. Kiss her until she admitted that she felt the sizzle between them as intensely as the first day they'd met.

Had she felt the magic between them? She was certainly in a hurry to leave. Nothing he said even gave her pause to reconsider.

Was he losing his touch?

Nick swung into his suit jacket, savouring the sweet scent of her perfume still lingering on the fabric.

He rubbed the muscles in his neck. He had it bad. But then, there was nothing to say that he couldn't keep her for a while. Nothing at all.

He had been an idiot for accepting her leaving him in the first place. He should have put aside his work for a time and followed her, found her, convinced her that no matter what that other guy had said to her, they were right for each other.

He would have saved her from the pain of being betrayed. That jerk. Who would consider another woman when he had Skye?

He froze. Who would consider work instead of her? He rubbed his jaw. He should have spent more time with her. He wouldn't have lost her then. But he had been blinded—getting a job in one of Sydney's most prestigious law firms was an opportunity of a lifetime. He couldn't pass that up for anything. And he hadn't. And he'd lost her. And the pain was still with him.

Was it worth it? No. Yes. No. He didn't know. But he did know he couldn't pass up this chance now.

They could have some fun together. And she could be just what the partners ordered. Partying around with models was all well and good but if he wanted to project a responsible, stable air to potential clients an honest, steady woman in his life would be a good thing, for him and his career.

Perfect timing too for her to come back into his life, just when they were considering him for the promotion to senior partner.

If he had to go steady with someone he couldn't think of a better woman than Skye Andrews. And there was no way she'd have skeletons in her closet that would compromise him or the job.

She was perfect. And with no strings attached.

Skye rolled over in bed, draping her arm over the warm body beside her, nuzzling closer. She wanted to stay right there in bed, where it was safe and warm, where she was loved.

She'd hardly slept at all. She couldn't stop thinking about last night and that last kiss. Had she done the right thing in keeping the truth from Nick?

She touched her lips, careful not to wake her bed-mate. What a kiss it'd been, a kiss that she'd hold close to her heart in the years to come, a kiss that fairytales were made of.

She pulled the covers up higher, covering the bare shoulder beside her. It was all over. Nick would leave her alone now that he'd got what he had wanted, got the answers to why she had left him.

She hoped that was all he was after—it was all she could give. He was out of her life, for good. She just wasn't sure whether that was a good thing, or not.

Skye ran her fingers along the edge of the duvet. She'd made her bed, now she had to sleep in it, for better or for worse. She shrugged. It was probably far too late for the truth now anyway.

Maybe she should have given him a good reason to avoid her. She nibbled her bottom lip. It would have been her insurance policy in case he looked her up later when he got bored with the models.

She stared up at the ceiling, breathing deep and slow, her eyes burning. Maybe she could have given him a chance, should have taken longer with him to see if he had changed, maybe her fantasies of them having a happy ever after with a family in the suburbs wasn't totally out of the question.

She smiled. As if.

The alarm bleated. Skye reached out and slapped the clock. 'Time to get up, honey.' She shook the shoulder gently.

The lump in the bed rolled over and blue eyes stared up into hers. 'Have to, Mummy?'

Skye nodded, giving her daughter a soft smile.

'Hug?' Holly reached up her small arms.

Skye wrapped her in a warm cuddle. Nick didn't know what he was missing—the little kisses, the hugs, the magic of having your child crawl into bed with you in the small hours of the night after a bad dream… Hopefully, he never would.

She couldn't imagine him taking the news of his paternity well, or all her lies.

She let out a deep sigh. She probably wouldn't see him again anyway, except for the wedding. She had nothing to worry about. Nothing at all.

The papers in front of Skye did little to distract her from her overactive imagination. Her mind dished up endless scenarios, from being old and alone to falling into Nick's arms to Nick bursting through her door demanding custody of their child.

The knock on the door startled her. It opened.

'Nick.'

'I'm here to give my best man's speech,' he said smoothly, striding into her office.

Skye could only stare at him. He was dressed in a dark blue suit, a white shirt and a rich lavender tie. His hair was neatly spiked, his face clean-shaven and his eyes bright with purpose.

She ached. Her first impulse was to rush into his arms and taste his lips again. She shook herself. Crazy!

'To me?' she asked breathlessly. It was okay. Just breathe. It wasn't anything more than a speech. It was just doing her job. She could do that.

'To you.' His deep voice rumbled through her, with a hint of amusement. He moved to the seat opposite her desk, sitting down and facing her, propping his elbows on his knees.

She lifted her chin, ignoring the buzz in her veins. 'I'm just going to lunch.'

'I can go with you if you like.' He glanced at his watch. 'I don't have long but—'

She sighed. 'No, that's okay.' She gave the clock on the wall a cursory glance. 'It's fine. I'm fine. Go ahead. Do your speech.'

'Okay.' He stood up, lifted an imaginary glass and looked down at her intently. 'I'd like to offer my congratulations to Cynthia and Paul, my good friends, who've had the courage and determination to tie the knot. May your lives be filled with enough happiness to keep you both smiling, enough hope to keep you strong, and enough trials so you need a lawyer like me in your lives. I wish you both all the best and especially you Cynthia, who for reasons unbeknown to most of us here today, chose Paul to be your husband.'

Skye looked up at Nick, counting her heartbeats, taking each breath slow and deep. He looked amazing. Was amazing. How she was going to go on without even the dream of him in her life…

Nick sat down, crossing his arms over his chest. 'Well?'

Skye nodded slowly, buying herself some time. 'Really good, but at the end it sounds a bit like you want the bride for yourself. Not that there's much chance of that, but—'

Nick leant forward. 'All I could think about was you.'

'That's terribly romantic, if I was dumb and believed you.' She swallowed. What on earth was this?

He'd received his answers last night, so surely he was satisfied now and would leave her little life well and truly alone and get on with his own. She wasn't affair material—she wasn't tall, blonde, or a model.

'It's true. I haven't been able to get you out of my mind.' He ran a hand through his hair. 'And, believe me, I tried.'

'Oh?'

'I've got several big cases that need my undivided attention and all I can think of is you, and that kiss last night.'

'It meant nothing, Nick.' She sucked in a deep breath. 'Absolutely nothing. It was just two people saying goodbye. That was all.'

'I felt a lot more than that. And I think you did too.' He probed her face. 'And if you were honest with yourself you'd admit it.'

She bristled. 'Come on, Nick. I know a lot of things and the most important one is that you're a lawyer. Your life is manipulating words and people. So whatever you're after—'

'Lawyer jokes have a lot to be responsible for.'

Skye crossed her arms and glared at him. 'Right. Not one iota of truth in them?'

'A bit, maybe.' He shoved his hands in his pockets. 'But what are you saying? That you'll never believe anything I tell you because I'm a lawyer?'

She glared at him. 'No.'

He leant back and crossed his arms over his chest. 'Then what? You won't believe how I feel about you?'

'No. I don't.' She lifted her chin and shot him a

look of disdain. 'You have a flair for convincing the people around you what you'd like them to think. I figure this time you've convinced yourself as well.'

'How can I show you, then?' His eyes glinted mischievously.

Skye stood up and stepped back. This wasn't how it was meant to be. It was meant to be over. 'Nick. There's no future in us.' She waved her hand between them, acutely aware of the distance vanishing between them.

'And why not?'

'You're not into—' she spread her arms wide '—all this. Love, commitment, marriage.'

He shrugged. 'Things change.'

'Right. That's your story for now.' She strode to the door, steeling herself against the pain in her chest. 'But truly, whatever game you're playing here, you won't be happy in the long run.'

Nick stood up and followed her to the door. 'I'm not playing games, Skye. I felt something between us last night that I want to explore.'

Her heart fluttered. 'Well, I don't,' she said harshly. 'I've been there, done that. So have you.'

'It wasn't enough for me,' Nick said gently, staring into her eyes with his brilliant blue ones.

She crossed her arms over her chest. 'It took you four years to work that out?'

'I was an idiot. But here we are, now, together again. Let's not waste the opportunity.'

She shook her head vehemently. 'I'm not what you want, truly.' She cringed. Being 'saddled' with a woman and child would be the last thing he'd want for himself if he knew, and his father would hit the roof.

Skye could imagine his father's disappointment if Nick settled down with her. She'd met the man several times and had loved the way they related to each other, loved the way he cared about his son's life, no matter how extreme his views were. Nick had his father's love and she'd never jeopardise that.

She would give anything in the world to see the same adoration in her own father's eyes for her, but that would never be. Her father had left her mother when she'd been ten, not wanting to have anything more to do with any of them since.

Tara planned to see him on her European honeymoon next year. Her older sister was braver than she was! She'd had all the rejection she could handle.

'How can you know what I want?' He cupped her chin with his palm and leant forward, brushing her lips with his.

She pulled back. 'Please go, Nick,' she managed, her pulse pounding in her veins.

Nick felt the words like blows to his chest. She wouldn't even consider an affair? How could that be when her lips danced beneath his, when her body heated at his touch, when she melted against him when he took her in his arms? He frowned. She made no sense.

Nick stepped into the doorway, loath to leave without something he could work on. He turned back to face her, his breath like fire in his lungs.

'Skye, John's here to see you,' said the designer

sister breathlessly behind Nick, as though she'd just arrived—she hadn't been around when he came in.

Nick swung around. 'John?'

'Not that John.' Skye's voice was tight, coming close behind him.

Nick stalked into the foyer. The man who stood by the desk, a rose in his hand, looked exactly like the John Skye had described last night...

'Nick, no. Please.' Skye put a hand on his arm. 'I have to talk to you.'

Nick stalked towards the man. 'Are you an accountant?'

'Yes, I am.' John puffed out his chest. 'Do I look like one or has someone been talking about me,' he lilted, looking behind Nick.

He wasn't out of her life! She'd lied to him. It wasn't that she wasn't interested, it was that she was still in a relationship!

Fury pumped through his muscles. He clenched his fists, reducing the space between him and the jerk who had stolen her from him.

He dragged in a deep breath. 'Are...you...in...a... relationship...with...Skye?'

'I guess you could call it that.' He shrugged sheepishly. 'On and off.'

'On and off,' Nick repeated dully, the words slowly sinking into his brain. He swung to face Skye. 'You're still with *him*?'

Her wide eyes said it all.

Nick stalked to the door, wrenched it open, strode outside, dragging deep, slow breaths into his lungs.

She deserved better. Far better. And he was going to show her that, no matter what she said.

CHAPTER TEN

WHAT had she done?

Skye stared at John, her blood pounding in her skull like a jackhammer.

John's brow was creased, his gaze entirely on her. 'What in the blue heavens was that about?'

'I'm sorry, John,' she whispered. She was such an idiot! John didn't deserve this—curse her stupid mouth for her lies. The last thing he needed in his life was complications because she couldn't get hers straight.

Goodness, they'd only gone out five times, and that was over several months.

How was she going to look John in the face ever again when he worked out she'd been telling stupid stories about him, just to get rid of the man that happened to be the father of her child?

The front door swung closed with a thud that echoed with finality. She bit the end of her fingernail. She could let Nick ride with the misconception that she was back with the man that she'd left him for and have him out of her life, or she could do the right thing.

She hesitated.

Skye wrenched open the door and followed Nick's large form striding along the pavement. She couldn't let him think ill of John—he'd done nothing, let alone cheat on her with another woman.

She grasped Nick's arm, forcing him to a stop. She stepped in front of him and looked up at him, her mouth open, a reasonable explanation on the tip of her tongue.

She froze.

His mouth was pulled thin, a muscle in his jaw flicking, and his eyes blazed down into hers. By the look in them he was contemplating murder—hers or John's?

She dropped her hand from his sleeve, wrapping her arms around her chest and lifting her chin.

'Nick, I—'

'Don't say it. I don't want to know,' he bit out. 'If you want to carry on with a man like that—'

Her blood heated at the arrogance of the man, thinking she wanted his opinion in any way. 'And what if I am?'

Nick ran a hand through his hair, glaring down at her. 'How could you…put up with *him*?'

Skye shook her head at the venom in his voice. Oh, no. She should have seen that coming. He saw John as the enemy—the man she had left him for.

She couldn't let John take the brunt of Nick's anger. She'd seen what he was capable of and it wasn't fair to a man that she barely knew to deal with whatever Nick might dish out.

She sucked in a deep breath. 'Nick. I need to talk with you.'

He crossed his arms over his chest. 'So, talk.'

'Come with me.' She slipped her hand into his

warm one. The touch of his skin against hers and the innate strength in him made her ache.

She half dragged him to the nearest café, pushed him into a seat, resisting the urge to hold his shoulders for a moment more than necessary.

Skye sat down opposite him, taking several deep breaths, calming herself for what she was about to do. 'Nick. I—'

'I'm willing to forgive you for leaving me for John,' he stated dryly.

Her cheeks heated. 'You'll what? You'll forgive *me*?'

'You were obviously taken in by the shifty weasel. We both know it was a mistake.'

'A mistake? You arrogant jerk!' She leant back in her chair, half-tempted to get up and leave him there. 'Is that the only reason you think someone could possibly say no to you? What if he was the most caring, giving man in the world who was quite prepared to give the one that he loved the family she wanted? Was thrilled with the idea of being the father of her children and being there for them?'

Nick shrugged. 'But he wasn't, was he?'

She bit down on her anger. 'Neither were you.'

His jaw clenched, his eyes slightly narrowed. 'If he was, then you would have told me from the start that you were still with the jerk.' He leant his arms on to the small table, making the thing feel even smaller. 'So, what's the story? Did he take you back? Or was everything you told me a pack of lies and you've been with him this whole time?'

She swallowed hard. There was no backing out

now, not if John was to go about his life, unhampered by her silly stories, and she wouldn't put it past Nick to make his life difficult.

Skye picked up one of the packets of sugar out of the dish in the middle of the table and moved it from one hand to the other. 'I lied to you,' she said slowly, glancing at him.

He shot her a penetrating look. 'About what?'

She pressed her lips together. 'About John.'

'What about John exactly? That he broke up with you—I didn't think that could be the case.'

She shook her head, her chest tight. 'I didn't leave you for John.'

He frowned. 'What? Then who? When you told me you were leaving I demanded to know who and—'

'There wasn't another man.' She bit her bottom lip, placing the sugar packet in front of her on the table's smooth surface, staring at it. The enormity of the decision now pressing down on her... To tell him the truth—the whole truth or a bit of truth or no truth at all.

She pushed the sugar packet away from her, her throat tight. 'I couldn't...I couldn't stay with a man that didn't want a family, that didn't want kids.'

He stared at her. 'What?'

She crossed her fingers under the table. 'I couldn't waste my time on a guy who didn't want kids, okay. That's all. That's it. That's why I left you.'

He leaned back, his gaze on her as though he was sizing her up. 'You didn't leave me for someone else?'

'No.'

His face brightened. 'You didn't fall in love with anyone else?'

'No.' She couldn't help but smile at the change in him. It was as though a load had lifted from his shoulders.

Nick leant over and held her hands in his, his warmth thawing the fear in her heart. 'But you loved me, right?'

She nodded. 'I loved you, Nick.' She was careful to use the past tense so he got the message loud and clear that it was over. 'But I couldn't stay...I... You...' She stalled. 'My father left my mother when my sisters and I were young,' she blurted, trying to lay the groundwork for the truth. 'It was hard growing up without a father. It was hard seeing my mother cope on her own without a husband.'

Nick leant over the table, his brow furrowed. 'What are you saying?'

She froze up. She couldn't do it. She couldn't tell him about Holly. She had no idea what he'd do if he knew the truth. She couldn't risk it, and couldn't risk Holly if he decided to fight for her.

'I'm saying that...for me—' she looked up to the ceiling '—my dream was to find a man that loved me **dearly**, marry him in a gorgeous white wedding, have **a ho**use in the suburbs and have children with him.' **She** took a breath and met his gaze. 'You had your dream. I had mine.'

'But you didn't get your dream.'

Skye hesitated. 'Not yet.' She pressed her lips tightly together, her mind scrambling for a more reasonable explanation to her leaving him—he'd never accept just that she wanted kids. Why then? Why hadn't she talked to him about it? Why hadn't she considered wearing him down to her way of thinking? All the things she had told herself she should try back then, but she hadn't had the energy to coerce him into something he was adamant not to have, hadn't had the courage, or the time.

Maybe she had been wrong, keeping the truth from him. Maybe he could have handled it. Maybe he wouldn't have forsaken everything he had dreamed of to make things right. Maybe he *had* changed. Maybe he wouldn't have seen her pregnancy as a trap to get him to commit to her...

'And this John fellow is an option?' he asked gently.

She shrugged. 'I'm looking.'

Nick waved a waitress over. 'Could I have a strong black coffee. The lady will have a hot chocolate.' He stared at the black melamine surface of the table. 'You could have told me that's why you left.'

'Would you have let me go?' she asked, her heart aching. She so wanted to just tell him all about Holly, about how wonderful his daughter was, about her first tooth, her first step, her first word, but couldn't, the words stuck in her throat.

He shook his head. 'No. I wouldn't have.' He rubbed his jaw. 'We could have worked something out.'

'How?'

'We could have made a plan of some sort.'

'That included children, when? In ten years, fifteen, twenty?'

'Some time after my career got to where I wanted to go.'

'Have you got there yet?' she asked, her tone harsh.

He let her hand go and leant back in his seat, staring out the window. 'No.'

'No,' she repeated dryly. She'd been right to keep the truth from him then, and now.

The bustle of people outside and the chatter of patrons in the café did little to affect the silence between them.

It had been said. It was clear, for them both now, that a compromise was out of the question then, and probably just as much now.

He had his life and dreams. She had hers.

Skye sighed deeply, letting herself go, enjoying the few moments that she had dreamed of, Nick and her together, knowing she couldn't keep him, knowing right down to her very being that she'd made the right decision.

'Are you ready to concede to destiny?' Nick leant over and clasped his warm hands over hers. 'We've met again for a reason. Let's not waste it. I want to spend some time with you, go out with you, be with you, and see where it leads.'

She pressed her lips together, avoiding his deep blue eyes and the way they were shining with promises that her body knew so well and desired. 'We know where it'll lead.'

He smiled. 'Yes. I think we do.'

She swallowed hard. Her prayers had been answered, however belatedly. He was amazing. He was here. He was real. And he wanted her in his life.

She bit her lip. Pity she wasn't the free and single spirit he thought she was.

'I know you're not so sure. We didn't exactly break up under good circumstances. I'm sorry I was so angry with you.'

She nodded. 'I did say there *was* someone else,' she whispered. It would be a good time to tell him about the little someone else there was in her life…see whether he was serious about seeing where a relationship went with her or just in it for a fling.

A muscle flickered in his jaw. 'I assure you, there won't be a problem. We can keep it simple, if you like. No strings.'

'No strings,' she echoed, a chill sweeping through her.

Nick squeezed her hand in his warm one. 'Sure. A no-strings affair.'

'An affair,' she murmured, the words slicing through her chest like a knife. 'You want a no-strings-attached affair?'

'Of course,' Nick said easily, his eyes bright with bedroom promises. 'I wouldn't want to tie you down. You could keep an eye out for the man that'll fit your criteria, if you wanted. We'd be good together. Have a good time.'

'Have a good time,' she echoed.

Nick ran a hand through his hair. 'Will you stop doing that?'

'Sorry.' She lifted her chin, her throat tight. 'I just want to establish the parameters of this relationship that you're proposing. I'm not about to rush headlong into an affair with you without knowing the rules.'

He nodded, smiling as though he was a kid at Christmas. 'Ask away.'

She closed her eyes, fighting the sting behind them. Maybe this wasn't like it sounded, maybe he was afraid to admit commitment to her, or anyone.

'I'll have my life—' Skye gripped her cup tightly, waiting for him to respond. She mentally crossed her fingers and toes. Let him be considering a serious relationship. She knew it was against the odds, against what he was suggesting, against everything she ever knew about him, but hell, she had to ask.

'And I'll have mine.'

She nodded, her blood cooling in her veins and her body suddenly heavy. 'At night—'

'We'll go out to dinner, enjoy moonlit walks, and each other at whosever place we end up.' Nick took a gulp of coffee and smiled at her as though he'd offered her chocolate-chip ice cream.

'No sharing a place?' Her heart ached, but she had to ask. No desire for them to be anything more than the flings that he had with those darned leggy models.

'No.' He shrugged. 'Don't want to rush into that sort of thing again. Maybe later, if everything is working out…but on the same basis, of course. No strings. I won't stand in the way of your dreams.'

She nodded, her mind numb. 'I get it.'

'So your answer is?'

She shook her head, struggling against the sting in her throat and the moisture in her eyes. She wanted to scream. She wanted to pick up the sugar bowl and throw it. She wanted more. She wanted it all. A lover, a friend, a commitment to a happy-ever-after. 'I...I've got to...think about it.'

'Then I'm not irresistible?' he teased, a smile tugging at the corners of his mouth.

If only he knew. 'I have to get back.' She took another gulp of the hot chocolate and jerked to her feet. She couldn't stand another second in his company knowing all he wanted was a different flavour of fling to his norm.

Nick stood up, taking her by the shoulders and drawing her closely to him. He brushed his lips across hers, sending a tingle of sensation coursing through her.

She resisted, steeling herself against what he evoked in her, holding on to the sad and awful fact that he'd never be her child's father, her life partner, her dream come true.

Nick pulled back. 'What's wrong?' He lifted her chin with his finger, gazing into her eyes.

'Nothing.' Skye forced herself to speak normally. 'I'm flat out at work, that's all. More work to do than there are hours in the day. You know how it is...'

And it took everything out of her to be so close to having it all and then losing it. Like last time round. She'd loved him enough to walk away.

This time she had to run.

CHAPTER ELEVEN

HE WAS an idiot.

Nick clenched his hands by his sides. What had possessed him to ask her outright for a relationship like that? Hell, he never had before with a woman. Sense had obviously eluded him.

He ran a hand over his jaw. He usually let nature take its course, and usually it didn't lead anywhere. Commitment wasn't his strong suit, or the women's, especially when they figured out they had no more in common than being the opposite sex.

He'd totally botched it.

It wasn't as if it mattered if Skye found someone else. He clenched his fists by his sides. He just wanted to get her out of his system...and these little dates did nothing to ease the tension in his body. In fact, they made it worse.

His idea that she'd be falling into his arms had gone awry. He'd half-expected her to melt into the woman he'd first met at his sweet gesture of flowers and chocolates. Thought she'd be totally enamoured with him after their dinner date. Had expected some response to his proposal today...

Nick turned on his heel and stalked towards the car park out the back of the boutique. John had been a surprise. Even if he wasn't the jerk who had stolen her from him—and he couldn't believe that there hadn't been a man—he didn't want him hanging around Skye.

John was the last man in the world for her. The man looked like the most boring, conservative man in existence—an accountant. He looked it. How could Skye even consider him? Sure, he'd have a stable income, be predictable and would give her the house in the suburbs with the yard out back and probably all the children she desired. But hell. She couldn't pick him.

He strode to his black BMW. He had to change tack. He'd charged back into her life like a bull in a china shop and he was making a giant mess of everything. He had to slow down. Romance the woman until she forgot about commitment and children and only thought about him.

He rubbed his jaw, a smile creeping on to his face. He'd find out the truth about her leaving him. There was no way that she would have sacrificed what they had shared together for the dream of having children some time in the future. Hell, she'd been twenty. There had been plenty of time for that later. It had to have been another man. And he'd find out about that thief and crucify him.

He knew what he wanted. He wanted Skye. A few weeks with her and he'd be over her and could get back to his life, clear and free of her.

Skye Andrews wouldn't know what hit her.

'Look what's just arrived for you.' Riana swept into Skye's office with a single yellow rose in a plastic barrel, tied around the middle with matching ribbons.

'From John?'

Riana shook her head, biting her bottom lip, trying to smother the smile creeping on to her face. 'No. Would you like to guess again?'

Skye let out the breath she'd been holding. 'Nick.'

Riana nodded, handing the flower to her as though it was the royal jewels themselves.

'Maggie still sick?'

Riana nodded. 'Yes. Sorry I was late in. I had a hot date last night.'

Skye nodded, taking the flower and rotating the tube. She knew the feeling. 'Have we got a spare vase? I'd like to get it out of this.'

Riana grinned. 'U-huh.'

Skye stood up and stalked out of her office and down the hallway, vividly aware of her sister following her. 'I can manage on my own now.'

'No, you can't.'

Skye darted a look at her younger sister. She was right. She didn't want to be alone and she didn't want to do it alone. All the more reason to ignore Nick Coburn and find a nice, quiet man to settle down with.

Riana followed her into the kitchenette, leaning against the bench. 'You know, this receptionist stuff is really cool.'

Skye took down a long smoked glass vase off the shelf and filled it with water. 'How so?'

'I'm not alone, you know. I like being in the middle of everything, watching everyone go past, hearing everyone's problems and helping you with your love life.'

'You sound like Mum.' Skye ripped open the cylinder and pulled out the perfect rose. 'And this is not my love life. This is a mess.'

Riana shrugged. 'At least it's not a flower-shop's worth.'

Skye put the flower in the vase. 'Yes, but somehow this seems scarier.'

'How?' Riana fluffed up her short dark hair with one hand. 'Why?'

'His gesture the other day was extreme to the point of showing off. An expression of comic grandeur that couldn't be taken seriously. This…' She drew the vase closer to her and rotated it, admiring the soft beauty of the single rose. 'This is seriously dangerous.'

'I don't understand.'

Skye waved a hand dismissively. 'Maybe I'm reading more into it than I should.' Maybe because she wanted to. Maybe she wanted him to want her, wanted him to seduce her into saying yes to his offer so the secret that lay heavily in her chest could be brought out into the open. She couldn't hide his daughter from him for ever, especially if they were having an affair.

Her blood warmed. An affair with Nick Coburn. Kissing Nick Coburn, running her hands over Nick Coburn's body, loving Nick Coburn absolutely and thoroughly. Yes. Oh, yes. Please.

She picked up the vase and dumped it in the middle of the table. No. She couldn't succumb to her desires, these wild thoughts of her and Nick, not when she had Holly to consider. And what on earth would Nick do if he found out the truth?

'A little danger never hurt anyone,' Riana said softly, a smile tugging at her mouth. 'Oh, and I need to leave early today, Skye.'

'Another hot date?'

Riana nodded. 'I really have a good feeling about this one. He's so cute, and so nice and so...'

Skye nodded. 'Sure. It's great that you're helping out in reception—we could get a temp in if you're too busy?'

'And miss out on all this?' Riana pointed to the single rose on the table, the bouquet on the bench and the stack of boxed chocolates on the top of the fridge. 'No way. Oh, and Tara's already left to supervise the Tate wedding. Is it okay for you to lock up?'

'Sure. I really need to stay and finish working on the Donovans' wedding plans—they've decided to go with us. They're coming in early next week to discuss them.' She walked to the doorway, biting her lip. Then there were the details that she had to review for the Harrison-Brown wedding to ensure she had it all under control. She hoped her mother would be back soon so she wouldn't have to face *that* wedding on her own.

'You should get Maggie to help.' Riana picked up the vase with the single rose and strode down the hall. 'Not right now, obviously, but in general. She could help you out while Mum's sick—and we all know how much you want to get home and be with Holly.'

Skye opened her mouth. Of course! Why look all over the city for another wedding planner whose loyalty could be suspect—they couldn't afford to lose any clients if the planner decided to branch out on her own. They could train one up themselves. 'She could be my assistant…'

Riana walked into Skye's office and placed the vase on the corner of her desk. 'Yes.'

Skye followed. 'With a little instruction she could easily fill the position of my assistant, helping me with the bookings and organisation of the weddings. And who knows, she may become another wedding planner in time.'

Riana spun and faced her, grinning. 'That would be wonderful. She'd love that.'

'Don't tell her yet. I'll talk to Tara first thing tomorrow morning, but I'm pretty sure she'll think it's a great idea too.' Skye couldn't help but smile. And situations like this wouldn't happen again. They would have Maggie to take up the slack if anyone got sick or was out of commission. If only they'd thought of it sooner…

Riana straightened taller. 'I'll hardly sleep a wink tonight with the excitement of telling her. Could I be there when you do?'

'Of course. I hope she'll be coming in tomorrow— I sure need her up and running tomorrow if Tara agrees.'

'She will.' Riana held up her hands, crossing her fingers and inching backwards out of the door. 'Goodnight, Skye.'

'Night.'

Skye bent over the papers, checking off the details, adding the latest notes into the files, including all the changes that invariably occurred along the way.

She couldn't help looking at that darned single yellow rose every time she lifted her head to think. Was that Riana's idea—to keep Nick on her mind...? It was working.

What was she going to say to him?

'You should lock your door,' a familiar deep voice said quietly from her doorway.

Skye jerked her head up. 'Nick.'

He walked slowly into her office, his hands behind his back. 'It's after seven and you still have the front lights on and the door unlocked.'

Darn. She stood up, her heart pounding in her chest. 'I must have lost track of time. What are you doing here?'

'I was passing...' He held up two carry bags. 'Are you hungry?'

The scents of Chinese food wafted towards her, sweet and spicy, rich and tempting. 'Maybe. What'll it cost me?'

'Nothing, I assure you.' His eyes glinted as he raked her boldly with his gaze, down over her white shirt, over her plain black trousers, to her black heels and up again, his gaze resting on her lips. 'Okay, maybe it'll cost you...a kiss.'

She shrugged, ignoring the flutter in her belly. 'Sounds steep.'

He raised an eyebrow. 'Am I that bad a kisser?'

'No.'

'Then...?'

She moved towards the door. 'It's what happens after I've kissed you that might be a bit of a concern.'

Nick dropped the bags on to the coffee table and sat down on the sofa. 'You mean when you're hopelessly addicted to me… There are special centres you can be admitted to for a cure, but it's long and painful.'

'I know.'

Nick's blue eyes widened. 'You know?'

Skye's mind buzzed. She could see what he was thinking and it was the last thing she wanted on his mind. She didn't have feelings for him. 'I read the papers.'

'Oh.' Nick laid out the contents of his bag on her coffee table, opening the containers and the bag of prawn crackers. 'I assure you the reports of my exploits have been grossly embellished.'

'Sure.' She pointed to the hallway. 'I just have to go and lock up—' Accepting she was hungry was one thing, getting her body to move closer to the man who had turned her life upside-down, another altogether.

'All done. I took the liberty as I passed through.' He smiled at her.

Her body tingled. She forced herself to look down the hallway to the dark and shadowy foyer. He had. She was locked in with Nick.

She sucked in a deep breath, moving closer to the sitting area. 'Did you come for an answer to last night's question?' she blurted.

He shook his head. 'I came to apologize.'

She opened her mouth but no words would come out.

'I didn't mean to put you on the spot. I just said what came into my head. You don't have to give me an answer. I shouldn't have asked the question. I just got carried away.'

'I find that hard to believe.'

'Me too.' He shrugged. 'But still, I spoke hastily.'

Skye stiffened. 'You don't want an affair with me?'

'Sure I do.' Nick smiled at her, his blue eyes bright. 'I just shouldn't have said it straight out like that. It was very unromantic of me.'

She held her hands tightly in front of her. 'And no-strings affairs are romantic?'

'Sure. Especially if you don't lay down the rules as callously and carelessly as I did with you. I'm sorry.'

She moved to the far end of the sofa, staring down at the food laid out, focusing on the hollowness in her stomach not the emptiness in her heart. 'But then no one gets hurt by any misconceptions they might have.'

'Absolutely.' He nodded and sat taller. 'That's what I thought in the first place. I thought you'd want it straight up, no sugar-coating.'

Skye sat down heavily, close to the arm of the sofa, as far away as she could from Nick. 'Pity you don't give your models the same consideration.'

'Ye—es.' He unwrapped a pair of plastic chop-sticks.

'But I'm not one of your tall, blonde models, am I?'

'No. You're not.' His voice was deep and thick.

She picked up the container closest to her, the scent of sweet-and-sour chicken filling her senses. Her favourite. 'Do you have a little black book on all the girls you date?'

He handed her the chopsticks. 'No. Why?'

'Sweet-and-sour chicken is my favourite.'

He smiled softly at her. 'I know.'

'But how?' Her blood rushed to her ears. 'If you don't have a book—'

'I remember,' he said gently.

'Oh.' Her cheeks heated. 'What else do you remember?'

'Everything.'

Her grip tightened on the container. 'Everything?'

He nodded, picking up some vegetables with his chopsticks and putting them in his mouth. 'Everything except knowing that you did all this.' He looked around the room.

She snagged a piece of chicken with her chopsticks and popped it in her mouth, watching his gaze drift around the room. He'd think it was all overdone, from the white sofa with red heart cushions to her white desk to the shelves on the walls covered in wedding favours, examples of invitations, glasses, champagne flutes and even the little couples that topped the wedding cakes.

'You must be good.'

She swallowed. 'Why do you say that?'

He shrugged. 'Because you have such a kind heart…' He took a prawn cracker and bit it, chewing thoughtfully. 'Although it baffles me how you could have told me there was another man and there wasn't.'

She snagged another piece of chicken. 'You don't believe me?'

'I didn't say that.'

She eyed him. 'Then what are you doing here?'

He looked at the spread on the coffee table. 'Feeding you.'

She put another piece of chicken in her mouth, glaring at him. How was she going to work out what on earth he was up to, what he really wanted, when he could talk her in circles whenever he wanted to?

Nick took another scoop of his dish. 'I hope you're not just picking the chicken out of that mix, like you used to do.'

Her stomach tightened. 'Will you stop doing that?'

He chewed slowly, his attention on her, finally swallowing. 'What?'

'You know what. Stop remembering me the way I was.' She didn't want to think about him caring so much for her, that she'd left such an impression on him. It made everything so much harder.

'Why? You were beautiful.' Nick looked at her, his blue eyes soft. 'I thought I was the luckiest man alive to have you in my life.'

Skye shifted in her seat. 'You did?'

He put the container he was holding and his chopsticks down on the coffee table, facing her. 'I'm sorry I didn't show it more. Tell you. I was young. I was scared of what I was feeling.'

She lifted her chin. 'Really, and what were you feeling?'

He moved along the sofa, reducing the distance between them. 'I loved you, Skye. I honestly loved you.'

She shook her head, her chest aching and tears stinging her eyes. He probably didn't even know the meaning of the word. Probably only used it as a line…if he'd really loved her she would have been the most important thing in his life, not work, not his career.

He nodded, moving his arm along the back of the sofa.

Skye sat frozen to the spot. 'Don't, Nick. Please.'

He reached up his other hand, running his palm down the side of her cheek, his thumb tracing her cheekbone, her lips.

Skye closed her eyes, her body still, her heart pounding against her ribs. Could this *really* be happening? Could he really have loved her? Could she trust him?

Or was it all a game?

CHAPTER TWELVE

HE BRUSHED his lips over hers. 'You said you loved me too,' he whispered, cupping her face with his hands.

A shiver of wanting ran through her. 'I did.'

'Then it had to be hard for you to have left me the way you did,' he said, pushing back the stray wisps of hair that escaped from the clip at her nape, caressing just below her ear with his thumb.

'Yes,' she whispered, the heat from his touch radiating down and through her body, kindling the fire deep in her belly.

Nick leant forward, pressing his lips to her neck, where his thumb had been. 'You would've had to have a damned strong reason,' he whispered, his hot breath against her ear. 'Or you would have stayed with me.'

Her skin prickled with pleasure, the sensation racing down her spine and deep into the core of her being. 'U-huh.'

He trailed his hot kisses down her neck, moving even closer to her. 'It had to be there and then.'

She nodded, relaxing in his arms and closing her eyes to savour the undeniable magnetism of Nick, his touch and his lips.

'So, tell me,' he asked slowly. 'Who was it that you left me for?'

His words spun through her like a ricocheting bullet. She flicked her eyes open. 'So that's it,' she croaked, her voice deep and husky. She cleared her throat. 'You didn't believe me...it *wasn't* another man, Nick.'

'Swear to it.'

She lifted her chin and stared him right in the eyes. 'I swear, Nick. It wasn't another man.'

His gaze searched her face, the intensity behind his blue eyes as obvious as the muscle quivering in his jaw. He shook his head. 'I don't understand.'

She jerked to her feet and strode across the room, as far from him as she could. She stared out of the window. 'So, that's what all this was about. You just wanted to clear the ''other'' man issue up.'

'No. I want to be with you, Skye,' he said close behind her, too close.

His gentle touch on her shoulders, the velvet warmth in his voice, sliced through her. She spun around to face him, dragging in a deep breath. 'Sure. Fine. Whatever. You want to know how hard it was to leave you?' She glared at him. 'Fine. It nearly killed me. Happy?'

'Then why?'

She stiffened. 'I told you why.'

Nick shook his head slowly, his eyes not leaving hers. 'It doesn't make sense. Nothing makes sense. You're driving me mad, Skye. I like having everything explained, having control of my life and since you left me—'

'Tough. Life's like that. Get over it,' she said

loudly, the words strange on her tongue. He was all she'd ever wanted...

He crossed his arms over his chest. 'You're not going to tell me the truth about that day then?'

'You can't handle the truth.'

'So it *is* another man?'

'No.' Skye walked to her desk and straightened her papers. 'Not another man, Nick.'

'Then what? Who? Tell me,' he demanded gruffly.

She shook her head, staring at the single yellow rose in the vase on her desk. 'When you grow up, Nick.'

'What?' He advanced towards her. 'What in hell is that supposed to mean?'

Skye picked up a folder and hugged it tightly to her. 'When you stop running around after anything with breasts I'll tell you about that day, about why I really left. Until then...'

'You don't trust me?'

Skye pushed past him and yanked out a drawer on the filing cabinet. 'You're a self-confessed playboy. What is there to trust, Nick?'

'You know me, Skye. The real me. The last four years have been...crazy.'

She shook her head, shoving the file into place and turning to face him. 'I don't know, Nick.'

He ran a hand through his blond hair, staring at her as though he was warring with himself. 'Then know this.' He stepped forward and swept her into his arms.

The kiss was urgent, the strong hardness of his lips claiming her mouth, devouring her softness, shooting bolts of desire down her spine and into every nerve in her body.

He buried his face in her neck, breathing hot kisses against her skin. 'The rest…I'll show you…the magic we can have together.'

Skye swallowed hard, trying to slow her heart, still the fire that was burning hot and fast for him. 'I don't know if you're being real—' she sucked in a deep breath '—or playing a game with me Nick.'

He didn't know either. But having her in his arms, feeling her lips beneath his, feeling her arms around him…it didn't matter.

'Please go.'

He pulled back. Her eyes were wide, her cheeks flushed, her body stiff.

He hesitated. What? Leave? When every inch of him was aching for her? When she was so obviously yearning for him too?

He didn't understand.

Whatever the hell had really gone on four years ago while he was busy with building his career was the answer. He just had to find out what it was. Then he'd romance Skye Andrews until the only man she ever thought of was him.

Nick forced himself into action. It took all his effort not to pull her into his arms and just hold her.

He strode to the door, dragging long slow breaths into his lungs. She needed a bit of space, that was all. To think about him and his offer…

The hallway was shadowed, the foyer deathly quiet. He flicked the catch on the door and wrenched it open, striding through without looking back.

He made it to the kerb before he turned, the door just swinging back into position. She hadn't locked it. Dammit.

He stalked across the street to his car. He'd wait and watch out for her. He couldn't let anything happen to her.

He dropped down into the driver's seat and gripped the wheel tightly, his chest aching.

He wanted her. And, no matter what, he was going to have her. It didn't really matter what surprises she threw his way. Why she really left him. He wasn't about to let her slip through his fingers again.

Something had changed.

He could have made his move. She was obviously shaken, moved and stirred, and confused. It would have been easy to wipe her concerns away with his kisses, caress her body into submission and make passionate love to her. But he wanted more.

He stiffened. Hell, he might even love the woman. Maybe as much now as he ever did. He just didn't know what to do about it.

CHAPTER THIRTEEN

SKYE burst through the front door of her terrace house. It was so good to be home.

The house was a good size for now. Cute and cosy, but it would be nice to get a house with a bigger yard. A yard big enough for children to run and play in.

'How was your day?' Chloe sat on the living room sofa, her homework spread from one end to the other, the cartoon programme blaring on the television.

It was fantastic to have Chloe around to look after Holly after the sitter had left. Having a university student as a boarder kept her in touch with what life was like 'out there', without all the cares and worries she had.

'Great, Chloe. Just great. Do you like chocolates?' She dropped several boxes on the hall table and flung her bag on to the end of the staircase rail. She hadn't heard a squeak from Nick since last night and she was torn between relief and disappointment.

Was he thinking about growing up? Would he work out that his life wasn't as full as he wanted it to be and put his career aside for one minute and consider becoming serious about commitment, her, and children?

Wishful thinking. She knew his father. Knew his connection with him, knew his father's desperate need for at least one of his sons to achieve what he hadn't.

109

He was probably thanking the heavens in his escape from her. That was more like it. Or would be, if she told him about Holly.

'Are you going out again?' Chloe's tone was wistful. 'I wouldn't mind sitting Holly if you did.'

Holly looked up from the cartoons. 'Mummy.'

Skye turned, bending down and opening her arms for her daughter. Her little girl's dark hair was in pigtails, swinging madly as she ran forward into her embrace.

Skye held tight. What she did was for her, for them, for their future, and for her sanity.

Could she accept Nick's offer of an affair without strings? At least have him in their lives, let Holly know her father and take the risk that he would leave them. *If* he stuck around at all after he heard the news of his baby.

She let Holly go and stroked her hair, running her hands down her black locks, over her smooth cheek, looking into her blue-blue eyes, so like her father's. Her chest ached. Would Holly cope with the rejection? Would *she*?

She'd survived Nick Coburn once…

'We made cookies.' Holly's blue eyes were bright. 'We left one, Mummy. Eddy ate it.'

'That's okay. Ginger cats must be hungry a lot. Didn't he eat my piece of cake yesterday?' Skye had to smile. Chloe's cat sure loved the sweet things.

Holly nodded, holding on to her overall straps and grinning.

Skye kicked off her shoes. 'Did you feed him his dinner yet?'

Holly nodded proudly, lifting her chin and throwing out her chest like her father did. 'Fish.'

'Great.' Skye held her by her shoulders. 'And were the biscuits yummy?'

'Yep.' Holly grabbed her hand. 'Come watch the 'toons with me.'

'I'm sorry, baby, but I've got a bit of work to do and if Chloe hasn't got plans...' Skye raised her eyes at her boarder '...she'll be playing with you.'

Chloe nodded. 'Sure. I'm staying in tonight. Usual rates?'

Skye nodded. 'Absolutely.'

'Can I come work too?' Holly asked, her eyes wide and tilting her head on an angle.

Skye stood up. 'I'll be in the kitchen, honey. You can visit me when the cartoons are over and help me sort out my pens, and tonight we'll have...pizza.'

Holly clapped her hands, her blue eyes bright. 'Yay!' She pointed to the television. ''Toons are on.'

Skye was glad the cartoons were more interesting than seeing her change. She couldn't have coped with her following her every move just now. She had to think, and work, and exorcise Nick from her mind.

'What happened with that guy you went out with the other night?' Chloe got up off the couch and approached Skye. 'You didn't say.'

Skye stared after her daughter, watching her plonk herself down in front of the television, dragging the sleeping cat beside her on to her lap. 'Why do you ask?'

'You have this look on your face—'

She sighed. 'Well, he popped into the office with some Chinese takeaway last night.'

Chloe wrapped her arms around herself and grinned. 'Ye—es. And?'

Skye kicked off her heels, pushing them under the hall table. 'We talked, sort of, and—'

'And he kissed you, right?'

Skye sighed. Chloe was as good at reading her as her mother was, and Riana. She could be an honorary Andrews sister for the matchmaking gleam in her eye.

As for Nick kissing her…what could she say? Just thinking of that last kiss stirred the embers simmering deep in her body. Skye opened her mouth but the words wouldn't come.

'That bad, eh?'

Skye shook her head, smiling, the wave of desire flooding anew through her body at the thought of Nick and his hot lips. 'It was…unforgettable.'

Chloe grinned. 'That's the way to have them.'

Skye pointed towards the stairs, eager to get off the subject. 'I have to change and then do some work. You are all right to watch Holly? I don't want to mess up your plans.'

'No plans tonight except for watching TV.'

Skye climbed the stairs, a soft smile pulling at the corners of her mouth. Nick wanted her. Sure, on his terms, but he wanted her.

It was a great compliment. Was she being crazy wanting to have it all? Was it worth thinking about, even with his 'no-strings-attached' policy? Maybe it wouldn't be as bad as it sounded, maybe he'd realise there was more to life, maybe he wouldn't totally freak out about Holly, and fall as deeply and thoroughly in love with her as she was. Maybe, just knowing he was a father, he would reconsider...

She touched her lips, reliving the kiss he'd given her. The man that she loved was in her life again... Could their little family be complete?

It would mean telling Nick the truth, and she had no idea how he'd accept the one thing that he had been adamant on never having.

Was he worth the risk?

Nick stood on the doorstep of Skye's cute little Victorian terrace, a dozen yellow roses clutched grimly against his chest.

This was it. If he played it right he'd get to be with Skye in a way that he hadn't with any other woman in his life.

Being with Skye was all he could think about. Where it would go next he had no idea. He shook his head. He just wanted to keep her, somehow.

The thought of failing sliced through him like a knife. He couldn't lose her. Not again, not for anything.

He had the plan all worked out. He had to show her that he wasn't going to pressure her into a relationship. That he'd go with the flow.

He had to make her feel that she could still look for what she figured her perfect partner would be like, while he was convincing her that it was him.

He had to show her that, despite his need to concentrate on his career for the next few years, he could give her all the romance and commitment stuff she needed, in time.

He rapped sharply on the heavy timber door and counted his thudding heartbeats against his chest.

A small girl opened the door, barely a metre high, clad in teddy bear pyjamas. Her hair was in two dark plaits sticking out from her head at wild angles, all ruffled. Her eyes were big and wide, staring up at him as though he was an alien.

His chest tightened. 'I think I have the wrong house.' He stood back and surveyed the number hanging beside the door, the blood rushing in his ears. 'This is the Andrews' residence, isn't it?'

His gut twisted. He had to have the wrong house. Skye would have told him she had kids…surely. Everything out of her mouth couldn't be a lie? Was there a husband and half a dozen nippers inside, snuggled around the kitchen table eating toast and Vegemite?

A young blonde woman came up the hall, a large ginger cat in her arms. 'It's okay, Holly, I'll take care of it. Your cornflakes are getting soggy.' She looked up at Nick. 'I'm sorry. Who are you after?'

'Skye Andrews. Does she live here?'

'Yes, of course. It's her house. We just share with her, that's all.' She touched her chest with her free hand.

Nick let out the breath he'd been holding.

'I don't think she's up yet,' the young woman offered.

Nick nodded, brandishing the flowers in his hand. 'I'd like to surprise her. She really likes a guy being romantic.' Visions of waking Skye years ago came to mind, of her touch, her smile, her kiss. Of how he used to tease her awake with the petals of a yellow rose, and make mad passionate love with her in the morning sunshine.

The young woman eyed him as though with a new appreciation. 'You know her well, then?'

'Very well.' He reached out his hand. 'Nick Coburn.'

'Chloe.' The woman clasped his hand, tilting her head, a smile tugging at the corners of her mouth. 'You're that guy that she went out with the other night, the one who brought her takeaway at the office?'

'Yes. Did she say something about me, then?' He smiled, his body warming. He had made an impression.

'No, it was just the look on her face....' She opened the door wide. 'Go on up, then. First bedroom on the left.'

He slipped past the young woman and climbed the stairs. He froze at her open doorway. She was like a dream—lying in bed, her long, dark hair flowing over the cream pillows, her eyes closed—she looked like an angel.

His gut tightened. She was too good for him. He didn't deserve her. He was half-tempted to skulk back to his empty apartment and emptier life rather than take the risk.

He straightened tall. He hadn't backed down from any challenge in his life yet. He wasn't going to start now.

He walked slowly towards her, placing the yellow roses beside her on the pillow. He bent down and kissed her gently on her lips.

'Hmm, Nick,' she murmured softly.

His gut tightened. 'Skye,' he whispered, his voice breaking at the overwhelming pressure in his chest.

Her eyes flicked open. 'Nick! What on earth are you doing—' her eyes widened '—here?'

'It's okay.' He stood by the edge of her bed, wanting to wrap her in his arms and dispel the wild look in her eyes. Was she afraid of him?

She sat up and shot a look at the door. 'Did you...have you... I mean, how did you get in?'

'The lady downstairs let me in, her and her cute little girl... Holly with the plaits.'

'*Her* girl?' she echoed, pulling the covers up over her teddy bear pyjamas.

'Yes. What's the problem?' He shifted the weight on his feet, slipping his hands in his pockets.

'You're...you're—' she looked towards the doorway '—you're in my bedroom.'

He smiled softly. 'It's a sacred place, I know...' He rubbed his jaw. 'But I wanted to tell you that I've been doing some thinking—'

She sat up straighter and lifted her chin. 'Nick, there's more to life than just nice restaurants, nice cafés and sweet nothings. I've been thinking too, about your offer of an affair and I've decided—'

He held up a hand. He had to get the positives in and, by the look on her face, he could see she was damned uncomfortable about him being here. His blood cooled. Could that mean she meant to decline his offer?

He stood firm. 'I assure you there'd be no strings. You could see other men if you want,' he said cautiously, trying to figure out where he stood with her.

'And you'd see other women?'

'If I wanted, yes.' Not that he'd want to with her by his side. 'I don't see what's the problem here, Skye. You're obviously still single and you can't honestly tell me you're considering that accountant jerk.'

'Nick, you'd better sit down.' She gestured to the end of the bed. 'There's something important that I need to tell you—'

The door swung open and Holly charged into the room and leapt on to the bed. 'Want to play?'

'Holly, not now. Go downstairs to Chloe, please, and have your breakfast. I'll be down in a minute.'

The little girl stood up on the bed and stared at Nick, throwing out her small chest and putting her hands on her hips. 'Me Holly.'

Nick smiled at the girl. Her wild, dark hair stood at angles to her head, her pretty blue eyes looking him directly in the face. She looked more like Skye than that Chloe girl, with her dark hair and her olive skin, and the same teddy bear pyjamas too...

His gut tightened. 'My name's Nick,' he said softly, crouching, looking into the little girl's cute face.

He glanced at Skye, probing her eyes. She couldn't be *her* child. She would have said something, surely...

Skye was flushed, her lips pressed tightly together. 'Nick—'

It was in the tone of her voice. In the way she gripped the duvet. In the way her eyes darted from Holly to him.

Nick clenched his fists by his sides. Much as it killed him he had to go with his hunch.

'Where's your Mummy?' he asked the little girl, not taking his eyes off Skye's pale features.

The little girl spun around without a hesitation, threw up her arm and pointed to Skye. 'Mummy,' she announced proudly.

Nick felt her thrust in Skye's direction like a punch in the guts. He straightened tall, his mind in turmoil. 'The woman downstairs said ''we'' live here,' he accused. It couldn't be true...

Skye sighed. 'Her and her cat, Eddy, live here.'

'Right.' He ran a hand through his hair and took a step backwards, his mind running through the last few days, his body tense.

'I can explain, Nick,' she said softly.

'Really?' He clenched his jaws tightly together. 'Don't bother. It's obvious.' He turned on his heel and strode out of the room and down the stairs, taking three at a time.

Hell, it was so obvious now he wanted to slap himself in the head. She'd found someone to give her half her dream and she was looking for some other jerk to give her the other.

Which left him with nothing.

CHAPTER FOURTEEN

'NICK, wait.' Skye thrust the bedspread aside and pulled on a pair of her jeans, thrusting her arms into a jumper, wrenching it down over her head.

She hadn't wanted him to find out like this. It wasn't meant to be this way. She had dreamed of Holly being squeaky clean in one of her party dresses, of preparing Nick for the moment with soft words, strong hints, with extreme care.

She pulled the jumper down around her waist, over her pyjamas, her heart pounding in her chest, the guilt rolling through her mind. 'Holly, go to Chloe, okay?'

'No.' Holly's face was crumpled and flushed.

Skye hesitated. She looked to the door and then at Nick's child. She walked over to her little girl and wrapped her arms around her. 'It's okay, honey.'

Holly nestled her head in the crook of Skye's neck. 'Mummy sad?'

'I'm fine, Holly. Really.' The last thing in the world she'd wanted was for him to find out like this. Darn. This was the worse case scenario, and the fact that he couldn't get away from them fast enough sat like a rock in her chest.

She *had been* right in leaving him four years ago when she had discovered that she'd fallen pregnant.

How, she had no idea. They'd been pretty careful, but obviously not careful enough.

She'd agonised for weeks after she'd discovered she was pregnant with his baby. Whether she should tell him or not. He'd worked so hard to get where he was, was working so hard to go further, had dreams that couldn't possibly be reached if he had to support a wife and child so early in his career.

When he'd told her about his father's dreams for him, and his older brother's lack of drive, it became clear that Nick had taken it upon himself to carry the career torch for the entire family. Clear that she couldn't take that away from either Nick or his father.

She wished her father could have cared enough about her to stand behind her and encourage her to reach her goals. As it was, he was halfway across the planet with some blonde who had stolen him from her mother.

Skye hadn't been able to steal Nick's dream.

She had loved him so much that she couldn't let him make that sacrifice—she had known she had no other choice. She had wanted his child, regardless, no matter what that did to her own life.

She'd had her family. They had been there for her, Tara even leaving her job to bring them all together under one roof, taking on Camelot so Skye could look after her baby and still have an income.

Skye hadn't had any other choice but keep his baby from him entirely. She had known how dutiful Nick would be to his responsibilities, that he'd want to do the right thing. And the right thing would be totally wrong for him.

She hadn't let him sacrifice his dreams and she'd paid the price—no father for her child, no partner to share her life, and no complete family of her own.

She hugged Holly tighter. She'd been right not to tell him, but the thought did little to cheer her.

Tears slid unbidden down her cheeks. She sagged on to the bed, Nick's child in her arms. There was nothing else for it. What hope there'd been for them had well and truly gone.

This was how it was going to be from now on—their little family, broken and alone.

Nick Coburn slammed the door of his office and strode to his desk. Damn the woman. He couldn't get her out of his mind. The last few days had been filled with maddening thoughts, nagging questions and endless arguments with himself over whether he should ring her, see her, talk to her and find out what in hell had happened. Or to leave her well enough alone.

How could she? He sagged into his chair. She'd started the family that she had dreamed of while he'd been busy with his career, climbing the corporate ladder, and wooing tall blondes who had more time for the mirror than for him.

Skye's last four years had been filled with purpose, feeling the baby grow inside her, nursing the little one, nurturing her, watching her grow, watching her first steps…

He ran a hand through his hair, clenching his jaw. What had he expected? She always had a lot of love to give. He had been an idiot to think she'd keep it all to herself, that the last four years had changed nothing. Everything had changed.

She had a child. Hell. To who? And why wasn't he with her any more?

Was it the man she'd left him for? He banged his fist on the desk. Had she lied to him about that too? And that was why she had left him? Because she had wanted to go and have a baby with another man?

Nick leant heavily on his desk, covering his face. Where in hell did he stand now?

He had no idea where the lies started or ended. Why on earth would she tell him there was no one else when she'd had a baby? That bloke had to come into it somewhere…had to have meant something to her at some time or other.

He slammed his fist on the papers in front of him. He wished the damned investigator had got back to him before he'd run blindly into the disaster on Saturday morning.

Hell, the man had said he was busy, and Nick hadn't seen the need to hurry—and now, there was no point. Apart from knowing the name of the bastard who had impregnated Skye and left her to it.

'Mr Coburn, Sandra Baker is on the line. Is it a convenient time for you?'

'Absolutely,' he bit out. Anything to distract him

from his thoughts and this unpleasant pain in his chest.

'Nick, darling. What are you up to? Are you going down to the boutique for your final fitting on Friday?

Damn it. He'd forgotten all about the stupid thing. 'Sure.' He'd probably seen the time allotted on his schedule and tried to block it from his mind.

He didn't want to see Skye yet.

'It's been so nice, getting to know you and all with Cynthia and Paul's wedding. It would be nice to get together for a drink, some time, wouldn't it?'

He leant back in his chair. The leggy blonde might be just what the doctor ordered. 'Absolutely. How about we meet up after the fitting. Say five.'

'Great. I can't wait.'

'Me neither.' And, if he was lucky, she could take his mind entirely off Skye and prove that he didn't need her half as much as he thought he might.

He ran a hand through his hair. He'd been such an idiot. She wasn't just looking for a partner—she was looking for a father to that little girl of hers.

Nick snapped a pencil in half. No matter what she made him feel that couldn't be him.

The day dragged by. Nick could barely concentrate, with thoughts of Skye invading his mind. He'd run through going to Camelot early on Friday over a hundred times. But what would he say to her?

His gut tightened. What would *she* say to him?

He shook his head. He didn't want to hear whatever justifications she'd convinced herself of. So much for her dream of having a proper family. She was just like her mother—a single parent.

Nick rubbed the muscles in his neck. She deserved more. Who was the damned father? He wished he'd had more time to spend with his brother's children; he may have had an idea how old the little girl was and whether she was telling the truth about there not being another man when she left him, or whether she'd run into him later.

Hell. He hadn't got any answers by being with Skye, only more questions... How much more was there to know?

CHAPTER FIFTEEN

THE tuxedo fitted to perfection. The tailor had certainly done a great job. He'd tried to entice the man to make a few suits for him but the fellow had insisted that Camelot kept him busy, full-time.

He could understand that. They had quite a thriving little business for themselves. Even if Skye wasn't working full-time...and now he knew why.

Nick wrenched on his own suit jacket, straightened his blue tie and strode out of the fitting rooms.

'Nick.'

He looked up, meeting Skye's wide eyes. 'The tuxedo is fine,' he stated dryly. 'I have no complaints about the service here at Camelot or any concerns about Paul and Cynthia's wedding.' What had possessed him to agree to be best man, he had no idea. He'd never entertained being a part of the wedding charades of his friends before.

'Nick.'

Nick looked around the room, past the flower bouquets to the pictures on the walls. Framed photographs of myriad weddings dotted the walls—happy, bright faces surrounded by smiling friends and family. His body tensed.

He glanced towards the door, biting down on the question pressing in on him. It was hardly his business who Skye decided to bed down to sire her children. 'We have nothing to talk about.'

The last thing he wanted to hear were the sordid details of her relationship with the man who had given her that adorable child.

'How can you say that there's nothing to talk about?' Skye's voice was soft, pleading. 'There's so much to say.'

He shook his head and headed for the door.

She grabbed his arm. 'Nick, do you hate me that much?'

He looked down into her face, the pain of her words twisting in his gut. 'Hate you? Hell, Skye, I don't hate you.' He wasn't sure whether to pull her into his arms and hold her, wipe the creases from her brow with his lips, protect her from the reality of her life. Or escape.

She sighed. 'I'm glad, and I'm sorry, so sorry.'

He looked down into her face, her dark eyes staring up at him. Her skin, smooth and soft. Her full lips deep and red and inviting. 'I have to admit it was a surprise.' He cleared his throat, averting his gaze. 'It's the last thing I expected…'

Her grip tightened on his arm. 'I know but—' She dropped her arms to her sides.

He shook his head, crossing his arms over his chest. 'I can't imagine what you were thinking not telling me about her.'

Skye bit her bottom lip and her eyes glistened. 'We can still talk about this, can't we?'

Did she think he could still have an affair with her

despite her being a mother? He couldn't. For her sake or the child's. He shook his head slowly. 'Skye—'

She dragged in a deep breath. 'Holly needs her father.'

He stiffened. 'Sure, I can see that. But you could have thought about that years ago when she was conceived, right?'

'Yes,' she said slowly, her voice cracking.

Whoever the little girl's father was he'd sure be a fool to miss out on enjoying her childhood, missing that cute little smile and those wobbly plaits of hers.

'Yes, but it wasn't the right time —'

'And when would be the right time?' he bit out. 'If the bastard didn't have the sense to stay with you when you found yourself pregnant with Holly then what in hell makes you think that there'd be any right time?'

Skye stared at Nick, her body tensing. What was he saying? Was he saying he never wanted to know them? She'd tortured herself all week over his silence, not knowing if he was about to spring something on her or if he hated her for what she'd done.

Didn't he see she hadn't had much of a choice? Not knowing him, knowing his father, knowing his dreams and aspirations and how hard he'd worked. 'Nick—'

Nick moved towards the door. 'You should write the bloke off and find yourself a decent man who will give you the family you've always wanted.'

She dropped her hands by her sides, her throat aching. 'What are you saying, Nick? Are you telling me in some roundabout way that I can't count on you to even want to be a part of our lives?' Tears bit at her eyes. She didn't want that. She wanted to know him. See him. Be in some small way a part of his life again.

He stared down at her with his blue eyes, glassy and intense and cold.

'I didn't expect this,' she said softly, the pain of his chilly response slicing through her. 'I didn't expect you to turn your back on us.'

'It has nothing to do with me.' He waved a hand dismissively. 'Talk to her father.'

His words hit Skye full force in the chest. 'Nick. *You* are *her* father.'

His gaze pierced hers. 'What?'

Did he want her to spell it out for him or just to torture her some more? 'I had *your* baby, Nick. Holly is *your* little girl.'

'My little girl?' Nick echoed, staring at her with wide eyes, as though he could see the truth in her words in her face.

What was he saying? That he hadn't known? 'But I thought you knew…you saw her…' she said slowly, staring up at him. This couldn't be happening to her, not again. She'd thought they'd gone through all this back at her place on Saturday. She'd thought the truth had finally come out into the open, that he knew why she'd left him. 'You *were* there. You met her. You said you *got it.*'

Nick stiffened. 'I know there's a child,' he blurted. Hell, he couldn't take it in. His entire body was throbbing with the news. And heavy, as though someone had glued him to the floor and whacked him with a bat. 'I just figured she was someone else's…that whatever bastard you left me for had…'

Skye took a step backward. 'You idiot. Can't you tell how old she is? See your face in hers? That she's the right age for you to be her daddy?'

Skye's voice sliced through him. The mother of his child… She'd carried her, borne her, raised his little girl?

Nick's throat clogged with a warmth that he hadn't felt before. 'I don't…hang around children.' He ran a hand through his hair, his mind reeling. 'I'm a daddy?' The glow in the pit of his gut spread outwards. He stood taller. Could it really be true? 'You have to be kidding?'

Skye leant heavily against one of the chairs scattered around the room. 'You're really thick, you know that? Of course she's yours.'

Nick's heart thudded against his ribs. This couldn't be happening. Of course, it had crossed his mind over the years that there were risks to making love, no matter how much care he took. He just hadn't expected this, here and now. With Skye. 'There wasn't anyone else?'

'No. I told you there wasn't. I told you I lied. I did. I was pregnant with Holly when I left you, Nick.'

'Skye,' he whispered. She'd had his child…on her own. Without him. 'Why in hell didn't you tell me? Why did you feel you had to lie to me?'

Skye stared at the floor. 'I—'

He ran both hands through his hair, holding on to the roots. 'I deserved to know. I'm the damned father after all. Hell, Skye. I've been her father for what…?'

'Four years on the twenty-eighth of August.'

He set his jaw. She'd lied to him. Skulked away with his child and had her all by herself, to herself. And if he hadn't gone to her place he would never have known about her. 'Were you ever going to tell me?'

Skye's lips were pressed tightly together, her eyes cast down, her hands clenched tightly in front of her.

What in hell? Wasn't he good enough? Didn't he deserve to know? How on earth did she think he was going to accept this lightly?

'Nick, darling,' a woman's voice lilted. 'There you are.'

Nick swung around. Sandra. Her short black dress looked more suited to summer than Sydney's cool autumn days. Her hair was loose around her shoulders and her make-up heavy.

She moved forward without hesitation, giving Skye only the most cursory of glances, looping her arm around his. 'I can't tell you how I've been looking forward to tonight. I hear you have quite a reputation.' She chuckled, holding his arm tighter. 'Have you made reservations? Do tell me where?'

Skye's gaze was on him, her eyes wide and her mouth drawn thin. He knew how it looked. And she was right. This was him, what he did, who he was.

She knew that. Did a child really make a difference? Could he really acknowledge the little girl was his and disappoint his father?

He had no idea how she had even come about. Had a baby been all Skye had been with him for? She had been in an awful hurry to leave him…

Nick clenched his jaw. What game had she been playing? Why hadn't she told him? Why had she lied? Four years ago...or last week, or the day she'd brought the little miracle growing inside her into the world?

'Let's go then.' Sandra led him out of the boutique. 'I so love the colour of my dress. Did I tell you? It's the softest pink with lace in a classic style...'

Nick's heart thudded painfully against his ribs, his mind struggling with every step he took, leaving the mother of his child behind him without a backward glance.

For the first time in his life he had no idea how to handle a situation, least of all Skye.

CHAPTER SIXTEEN

SKYE sat at her desk, trying to smother herself with tissues, floundering as Nick's icy response to their baby shrivelled the last hopes of her dreams into a dull emptiness deep in her chest.

Nick knew Holly was his child and he'd ignored her, totally ignored her and, worse, gone off with that leggy blonde bridesmaid from the Harrison-Brown wedding.

She stared at the work in front of her, the words on the papers blurring. Typical.

She wiped her face and took several deep breaths. She'd expected him to have digested the facts during the last few days, to have come and had a discussion with her about their child. What had happened... Why she'd left... Why she'd kept the fact from him.

The last thing she'd expected was for him *not* to have got it. Adding two and two wasn't hard, especially when Holly had been standing in front of him staring up at him with his own blue eyes.

She pushed her now-cold chocolate drink away from her. He may be a pretty crash-hot lawyer but he was hopeless with this sort of thing.

Skye swallowed hard, dabbing her eyes with a tissue. It had to be a shock for him, becoming an instant daddy, but she still needed to tell him the reasons behind her decision, regardless of the tall, lanky blonde hanging off his arm.

She'd give him a bit of time to digest the facts, see her reasoning and sense. He'd come and find her soon enough, demanding to know the answers to the questions that had to be on his mind.

Another man…as if! He was the only man who had ever touched her heart, the only man in her life.

She wiped her eyes with a soggy tissue. Dammit. She sniffed and threw the tissues into her bin. He didn't deserve any more tears. She'd shed enough over the years.

So what, if she'd felt the weight of her secret heavy in her chest for the last four years. So what, if she'd fantasised about him finding out, coming to her and begging her to be part of his life again, seeing the gaping holes in his life. So what, if she was a total idiot for thinking he really would.

The blank look he'd given her when she'd told him he was Holly's father had spoken a thousand words, the blonde another thousand. He'd felt nothing, less than nothing. He'd arranged to meet the latest blonde in his life right here, under her nose, probably to rub her face in his total disregard for any sort of commitment.

Finding out Holly was his hadn't made a difference to him—he'd waltzed out the door with that woman without a hesitation.

She rested her face in her hands, leaning heavily on the desk. She had no idea what was going through his head, but he probably hated her now, and probably never wanted to speak to her again. The thought tore at her insides, filling her with dread.

She didn't blame him. He couldn't see it from her point of view yet. She'd kept his baby from him for *four* years, as far as he was concerned. Skye's belly tossed. And she'd fed him lies and avoided revealing her secret at any cost.

Her chest was tight, tears burning her eyes again. She just hadn't thought the cost would be so high. It had all sounded okay in theory, but seeing Nick again, kissing Nick again, being in his arms…

Couldn't Nick have acted like the mature adult he purported himself to be and have a sensible conversation with her and let the blonde down?

Hell. She thumped the desk with her fist. Now what? Would she get back to her life and pretend nothing had happened?

Impossible.

She jerked to her feet and stalked to the window. They had a rehearsal dinner for the Harrison-Brown wedding in three days' time. She'd be there. He'd be there. And, by goodness, she wasn't going to sit back and wait for him to make his next move.

His last one had said enough.

If Nick Coburn didn't want anything to do with them, fine. Skye chewed her bottom lip, lifting her chin. She was fine with that, as long as Nick didn't throw any surprises her way.

She just wanted her life back.

'You're awfully quiet, Nick.'

Nick clenched the wheel tighter. 'Sorry, Sandra.'

What was wrong with him? He had a pretty blonde beside him, who was keen to spend time with him, and all he could think about was Skye. And her child. Their child.

Dammit. He was a father. The thought evoked a deep response in his chest, a swell of pride, a lurch of excitement, and a dread.

Skye should have told him. Hell, didn't he deserve to know—then, and especially now? Damn, he wasn't the young fool that he had been then, consumed with work and himself. He was older. He was more responsible. He had work and a steady income—good prospects to raise a family.

Nick glanced at the blonde, struggling to make sense of it all. Being a father shouldn't change anything. It wasn't as if Holly didn't exist last week; he just hadn't known about her.

His life was normal.

Skye had tried, judged and sentenced him without him even knowing where he'd want to stand. He clenched his jaw. If he'd known he would have set down a case and a half supporting the motion of him being a part of their life, a convincing argument that she couldn't have refuted. *If* she'd given him the chance.

He ran a hand through his hair. He'd been such a young fool, mouthing off his opinions about commitment, marriage and families as though she was on his team, not a hostile.

What on earth gave the woman the right to run off on him and keep his child from him? That wasn't just.

Nick swung into the car park of the restaurant. He

couldn't fathom what she'd been through, carrying his child, bearing his child, bringing up his child. All on her own.

Why had she let him think it was another man for all those years…? Why had she let him carry such anger and bitterness over their parting for so long? He should have gone with his first plan and gone after her. Fought for her.

Nick would have found out the truth and made her his. Loved and protected her, supported her so she didn't have to juggle work with caring for their child.

Why hadn't she come to him? He could have made their lives easier, could have shared raising the little girl.

He clenched his jaw, fighting the pain rising in his chest. He would have liked to be there to hold his child as a newborn, would have liked to watch her first step, hear her first word, listen to her laughter…

'Was it a hard day at work?' Sandra lilted. 'Or were you having words with that wedding planner? I did sense a bit of tension there.'

He shook his head. He couldn't talk about it, could barely breathe for it. 'I don't think I'm going to be good company tonight, Sandra. Would you mind if I dropped you home?'

'Of course not. But I could help you push whatever it is bothering you from your mind.'

Nick turned the ignition off and turned to his date. There was no good reason why a good-looking blonde with nothing in common with Skye couldn't distract him now. It had always worked before.

He smiled warmly at her. 'That'd be great.' He

pushed open his door and alighted, slamming the door and dragging in deep, slow breaths. Nothing had to change.

He strode to Sandra's side and opened her door. She placed one long, bare leg out and then the other, reaching for his hand as she stood up, her skirt very short.

Her touch was nothing like Skye's.

'So, what's the problem? Work or something else?' Sandra raised an eyebrow.

Nick shook his head. 'It's nothing. Not worth wasting our energies on when I have a pretty woman like you with me.'

Sandra giggled, fluttering her lashes at him provocatively. Her black dress was tight on her stick thin body, nothing like Skye's womanly curves and full shape.

They strode into the restaurant, Sandra looping her arm in his as though she was staking a claim on him.

Would Skye ever want to again? Nick remembered their early days as though they were yesterday. Her soft dark eyes looking up at him with a brightness that had made his heart turn and his loins ache.

The *maître d'* seated them in a quiet nook in the softly lit room cluttered with small intimate tables for two. Candles flickered in small lamps on the tables, highlighting the deep red of the tablecloths and the pristine white of the china settings.

She lingered over the menu, shooting him coy glances. 'What would you recommend?'

Nick stared at her. There were no games like this

with Skye, not four years ago and not now. She knew her mind.

'I'm not one to recommend anything.' He hardly recalled the meals he had eaten here. He'd been here several times with one blonde or another.

'You're too modest.'

Nick ignored her. 'I'm going to have the soup, a steak and a chocolate mousse.'

He sipped his drink. Skye's favourite dessert was chocolate mousse. Hell, chocolate anything. She would have loved all those chocolates he'd sent her, was probably working her way through them as he sat here with Sandra.

Nick recalled vividly how she'd snuggle up in their bed, a box of chocolates on her lap, a soft smile on her lips, watching some romantic movie.

They'd been good times.

'So, tell me about yourself,' Nick asked, taking a gulp of his Scotch. Anything had to be better than torturing himself with sweet memories of Skye.

Sandra balanced her fork on her plate. 'Well...'

Nick tried to concentrate on the woman's words, on the tone of her voice, on the meal, on the ambience of the restaurant. But all he could think of was Skye. Her sweet voice, what she was doing, where she was and what his little girl was up to.

What was he going to do? Did he have to do anything? Hell, yes. There was no way he could pretend that Skye hadn't come back into his life for a reason, that discovering he had a child was for nothing, that he had an enormous decision staring him in the face.

He shoved another mouthful of his steak in his mouth.

Would Skye give him another chance? A man shouldn't be blamed for having strong views on issues such as children—ideas that were based on conjecture and not in fact. There was nothing to say he'd be like Robert and stall his career by having a child, as his father feared.

Nick put down his knife and fork, his gut churning.

This was impossible…his father would be mortified. The last thing he needed was another son to fall into the family way. Hell, it could kill him.

'I'm not boring you, am I?' Sandra wiped her mouth with the napkin. 'You haven't said anything in ages.'

'I apologise.'

'A difficult case?'

Nick nodded. 'Yes. A real tough case.' He'd dug himself a deep hole. He shouldn't have done such a good job trying to convince Skye he was all for having a fling with her. He'd have a tough time ahead of him to convince her otherwise.

The waiter arrived with the desserts. Nick took a mouthful of the silky smooth chocolate dessert. He'd been a fool to treat Skye like any other woman in his life. What must she think of him?

He stared over Sandra's head, taking another spoonful. He'd just have to sway her to his way of thinking.

Nick jerked to his feet. 'Are you finished?'

'Sure,' Sandra said smoothly, her eyes glittering.

The trip back to Sandra's place was like a lifetime,

Nick's mind scrambling through different angles to take in his argument with Skye, rehearsing his case, and laying down the evidence of his good standing and trustworthiness.

Nick pulled up at the kerb.

'Would you like to come up and have some coffee?' she lilted, her eyes glinting suggestively.

'Thanks. But no thanks.' Nick alighted and strode round to the passenger side, opening Sandra's door and holding it wide.

'Are you sure. I mean—' She slithered out of the seat, standing up right against him, pressing her body against his, pouting her lips and flicking her tongue across them, staring at his mouth as though he was on the menu.

'I know what you mean, and I'm flattered.' He stepped backward. 'But no.'

She stepped closer to him.

He slammed the car door and strode around his side of the car.

'But why?'

'I think I'm going to settle down.' Nick slid into the driver's side and smiled. And now all he had to do was convince Skye.

CHAPTER SEVENTEEN

'MUMMY play?'

'Soon, honey.' Skye opened the picnic basket and started packing up some of the remnants from their lunch, her heart heavy.

This was how it was going to be, then. Her and Holly, alone. She bit her lip. Until she found someone else.

She looked around her at the families at the picnic table, the children on the playground, the couples walking slowly along the path. Just the thought of seriously getting back in the dating game made her feel there was a steel weight pressing down on her.

The dates her mother had set up for her hadn't seemed real, not when her dream was still alive and vibrant, pulsing in her heart like a beacon of hope. Now, dates with strangers were all she had to cling to.

She passed Holly her bright pink plastic cup with some more juice and another chunk of bread. She would just have to get over it.

Skye snapped the lid off the salad container and scooped out an extra serving for Holly and for her. She would stay well out of Nick's way and do her darnedest to rid herself of his haunting memory.

He wasn't ever going to be her knight in shining armour.

Skye looked out at the happy people around her. She could be happy too, in time.

Her hand froze…a tall figure was striding towards them, his hair glistening in the sunshine. The familiar shape of his shoulders, the gait of his walk, the power in every step…Nick!

She gripped the container tightly, holding her breath, her mind a crazy mix of hope and fear.

'What are you doing here?' Skye's voice was tight. He looked amazing. Blue jeans hugged his hips and long legs, a simple polo shirt stretched across his wide chest. 'How did you know where—?'

'Chloe.' Nick shrugged. 'We need to talk,' he said casually, crouching down beside her without a hesitation.

Skye shook her head. 'Not here, not now.' She glanced at Holly, sitting wide-eyed on the picnic rug, looking up at Nick. She didn't want Holly to have to hear what he had to say about her.

'I'd love to join you, if I may.' He dropped on to a corner of the rug that was empty, behind Holly. 'I want to spend time with you two.'

Holly turned and faced him. 'Hi.'

Nick looked down at her, with a softness in his eyes. 'Hello, Holly. Are you having a nice picnic?'

Holly nodded her head, picking up a cherry tomato from the salad and biting down on it.

Skye's stomach clenched tight. 'Why, Nick?'

Nick swept out a present from behind his back and offered it to Holly. 'For you.'

'For Holly?' she asked, her blue eyes staring up at

her father as though he was Father Christmas himself.
She dropped the tomato and took the parcel.

'Yes.' Nick smiled.

'Nick?' What was he doing? What was he up to?
Had so much changed in the twenty odd hours since
the blonde had whisked him away?

He shrugged casually. 'For reasons out of my control I missed her birthdays— I don't intend to miss
any more.'

Skye's stomach tightened. She stared at Holly as
she tore open the wrapping, pulling out a white fluffy
horse.

'What do you say?' she prompted.

Holly glanced at Nick. 'Ta.'

'Do you like it?' Nick asked, the smile on his face
widening and the light in his eyes growing.

Holly nodded enthusiastically, dug through the picnic basket and started poking an apple on the horse's
nose.

Skye bit her lip, shifting in her seat. 'What do you
really want, Nick?'

'Why can't I just want this?' He looked around
him, over the families in the park, playing ball, eating,
laughing, over Holly galloping her horse in a circle
around her, over Skye, his gaze deep, dark and devastating.

She dragged in a slow breath. 'You...playing
happy families? Come on, you're kidding, right?'

Nick shook his head, his eyes not leaving her face.
'I'd love to.'

'Sure you do.' She put the juice back in the basket
and packed up the salad containers, the bread rolls

and the meats. 'Like you like getting teeth pulled. What's your game?'

'No game.'

'Right. I am talking to Nick Coburn here. The man that wanted to spend every spare minute of his day at work.'

'Skye, I just want to spend time with my child.'

'Why this one? Surely you have others...?'

He sobered, his brow creasing. 'No. I've been careful.'

Skye nodded to Holly. 'Not careful enough.'

'*You* were different.'

She tensed. 'Why?' She couldn't believe he was on the level. It had to be a ploy, a game, a plot of some kind...he couldn't be honestly interested in them. Nick and kids...no way. He'd told her often enough how he didn't want them, or strings, or duties that would take his focus away from work. And he was carrying on with tall blondes, for goodness' sake.

'Would you like me to push you on the swings?' He stood up and reached his hand down to Holly.

'Slide,' Holly said, sliding her hand into his.

Nick nodded. 'If that's okay with your Mummy?'

Skye watched as Nick's large hand enveloped Holly's. Father and child. She opened her mouth but no words would come, the warm ache in her chest taking her breath away.

Holly looked up at Nick then to her, a smile on her face. 'Horsey come too?'

Skye nodded. She watched them together, walking hand in hand across the lawn to the playground, Nick's head bent down, Holly's looking up.

This was what she'd wanted: Holly to know her father. But could he possibly be the sort of father that wasn't going to leave her high and dry? The sort that was going to be there for her when she needed him? The sort that would care what happened in her life? Or not?

Skye packed up the picnic. She couldn't do this. She couldn't play this game with Nick. It wasn't fair to her or Holly.

Holly climbed up the ladder on the slide. She pushed the horse down first, Nick catching it at the end of the slide.

Her fantasies of a happy little family were over. Reality was harsh but safer. She was a single mother, that was it.

Nick bent down and caught Holly as she got to the end of the slide. Holly laughed, a high, infectious laugh that warmed Skye down to her toes.

Nick bent close to her, talking to her, and Holly nodded and raced back across the grass. Nick followed, jogging slowly, keeping pace with Holly about two steps behind.

'I won!' Holly swung around, her hands on her hips.

'You are so fast,' Nick said, his eyes drifting to Skye's.

'Horsey hungry.' Holly sat down at the basket, opening the lid and scratching through.

Nick looked at his little girl, his eyes full of wonder. 'She's wonderful.'

Skye nodded. 'Yes. She is.'

He crouched down beside her on the rug. 'Skye...'

'How was your date last night?' she asked, sitting taller and looking out at the children playing cricket on the oval.

'Date?' He rubbed his jaw. 'It wasn't…it didn't… I—'

Skye raised an eyebrow. 'The great Nick Coburn is speechless?'

'I am human.'

'I have wondered.'

'Ha ha.'

Holly shoved a carrot under Skye's nose. 'Horsey eat carrot?'

'Yes, Holly, horses love carrots,' Nick said warmly.

Holly lay down in the grass with a stick of carrot and nuzzled the horse's mouth in the ground.

'I'd like to talk to you about why you kept this—' he looked at Holly '—secret from me. Didn't you think I'd be there for you?'

'I did, as a matter of fact. And that was the problem. I knew how much your career meant to you and the last thing you needed was a baby to think about.' And leaving him was the hardest thing she'd ever had to do.

A muscle in his jaw twitched. 'Shouldn't that have been my decision?'

She shrugged. 'Maybe.'

'So you made up that story about another man?' he said slowly and evenly, as though trying to control his temper.

'Yes. You jumped to that conclusion so I was

all for reinforcing it so you didn't have to worry about us.'

'I would have appreciated the chance.'

She sighed. 'And what would you have chosen?' Skye stood up, gathering the blanket.

Nick stood up and slid his hands into his pockets. 'I would have done the right thing. I would have married you, Skye. And given you a home.'

Her heart turned over with the fleeting thought of having been his for the last four years, of him sharing Holly's baby years, of them, being together and happy, and loving...' And the right thing was the wrong thing for you.'

Nick shook his head. 'How can you say that?'

'Easily.' She'd heard him say it often enough. How children were anchors for careers. How the last thing anyone needed when they were making their climb up the ladder was heavy baggage like children and partners around their neck.

Nick ran his hand through his light hair, his mouth pulled tight as though he was waging a war with himself. 'So you think you knew what was right for me back then? Then what now?'

Skye stared at Holly, chewing on the carrot with her stuffed horse. 'Well, I guess I'll see you in a fortnight.'

'A fortnight?' Nick echoed.

She nodded, picking up the picnic basket and straightening to her full height. 'Yes. Isn't that how visitation usually works, a day every two weeks?' That was all he could possibly want after that blonde episode...

Nick's eyes widened. 'Visitation? I wasn't thinking—'

'See you then.' Skye prompted Holly and took her hand and walked away, leaving Nick well and truly behind her. What else did he expect?

CHAPTER EIGHTEEN

'SKYE, there's a man at the door for you.'

'I'm not expecting—' Skye strode to the hallway, glancing out to the stoop. 'Nick. What are you doing here?'

He wore a black suit, the cut of the jacket framing his shoulders to perfection, his soft blue shirt and royal blue tie accentuating the deep blue of his eyes.

Her heart fluttered.

'I had a lovely time today with you both,' he said smoothly. 'And I'm here to take you out.'

Skye's breath caught in her throat. 'Why?' she managed.

'Because I feel we have a lot to discuss and it would probably be a good thing to do it privately, rather than in front of Holly.'

'Nick.' What could she say? It was a good idea, but after today she was hopelessly vulnerable to him. He was fantastic with Holly, attentive to her, totally what she'd dreamt and wanted for the last four years...

Holly stuck her head out from the lounge. 'Hi.'

Nick bent down. 'Hiya, Holly. What pretty pyjamas.'

'I got horse,' Holly said, thrusting the much-loved horse towards Nick.

'So you have. Isn't it about time for you to go to bed?'

She nodded. 'Read story?'

'Sure.' He straightened up and looked at Skye. 'I'll read Holly a story while you get ready to go out.' He stepped into the hallway and put his head around the corner, looking into the lounge. 'Chloe, can you possibly see your way to stay in tonight and keep an eye on my… Holly, while I whisk this beautiful woman off into the sunset?'

'Ab-sol-utely.' Chloe grinned.

Skye sucked in a deep breath. How dared he—?

Nick swung back to Skye. 'You said we needed to talk, so how about we take this opportunity?'

Skye sighed. 'Fine. Okay. All right.' She pulled out the clip at her nape and ran her hand through her long hair. Great. Just what she didn't need. Another dose of Nick on top of today's stirring little experience.

She clenched her jaw tight. So, he acted like a great father to Holly—there was more to it than a cute little stuffed animal and a stint on the slide. So, he was thinking they could be part of his life—it didn't mean anything more than visitation. So, he looked absolutely devastating in that suit and shirt—she could control herself. Or could she?

Nick's gaze was on her, fixed on her hand running through her long hair. 'And I think you'll agree… there is…a fair bit to…say.'

Skye dropped her hand. 'Yes.'

'Okay then.' He swung away from Skye and held out his hand to Holly. 'Take me to your bedroom.'

'I wish cute men like that would say that to me,'

Chloe chirped, coming out of the lounge and standing beside Skye.

Skye nodded. Her too... No! What was she thinking? That wasn't a possibility. Look what had happened last time round. She couldn't afford to let down her guard with him. She had no idea what he was up to.

'I'll help you choose something to wear if you like, while you're in the shower.' Chloe grinned. 'To save time.'

'Sure.' Skye nodded, going up the stairs. Clothes were the last thing on her mind.

She stepped out of the shower, staring down at the dress Chloe had set out on the bed for her. Long and black, with an asymmetrical hemline, form-hugging with fine shoulder straps.

She shrugged. It didn't matter what she wore. He had the blonde and she had Holly. She and Nick were mutually exclusive, never to be, jinxed.

She swept her hair back, swiped some make-up on and pulled on a silver wrap. She grabbed the matching silver bag and black heels.

She walked slowly towards Holly's room, Nick's voice smooth, deep and steady.

'And the prince bent down at Cinderella's feet and slipped her foot into the glass slipper. It fit perfectly.'

Holly was fast asleep. Nick got off the bed slowly, closing the book and laying it on the bedside table. He pulled the blanket up to cover Holly's shoulders and smiled.

'And they lived happily ever after,' he said softly.

'You don't believe that, do you?' Skye whispered.

Nick caught her gaze. 'Yes and no.' He reduced the distance between them. 'I think it takes a lot more work than it sounds, but it's possible.'

'O—kay.' She backed into the hallway. She hadn't expected him to say that.

He ran his gaze over her, down the form-hugging dress and up again. 'You look…good.'

She swung around and headed down the stairs. 'I didn't ask,' she tossed back at him.

'You didn't have to.'

Chloe looked up from the TV, a dozen books and papers around her. 'You two have a nice time. I won't wait up.'

'I have my mobile if you need me,' Skye said as casually as she could, ignoring the insinuation, her cheeks heating.

Chloe gave her a wink and a wave. 'Sure thing.'

'Goodnight,' Nick offered, coming up behind Skye, his cologne drifting softly to her senses.

'Night.' Chloe waved.

Skye strode after Nick to his big black BMW. He opened the passenger door and she got in. He shut the door behind her and moved around to his side.

Nick slid in behind the wheel, pushing the key into the ignition and firing the car to life. He worked the gears, his strong hands reminding her of how they'd once moved over her.

'You're doing well,' she said in a rush. 'Nice car.'

He accelerated. 'Yes.'

'I wasn't asking because I want anything from you,' she blurted, feeling the burn in her cheeks.

He changed gears. 'I know.'

Skye stared out of the window. She shouldn't have come. She could've got Chloe to work upstairs in her room and stayed in her own home, on her own turf, with Chloe and Holly around, just in case.

She didn't want anything to happen. She had enough problems, the least of all the pulsing ache deep in her loins whenever she was close to him.

The streets passed in a blur. Wherever he was taking her was close to the heart of Sydney. He pulled the car to the kerb.

Skye looked up at the large concrete building. 'Where are we?'

Nick stepped out of the car. 'My place.' He strode around to her side of the car and opened the door. 'I figured it was the best place for our talk.'

She raised an eyebrow, frozen in her seat. 'You really think I'm going to fall for that line?'

Nick crouched down beside the car. 'Skye, you're the mother of my child. You've got to start trusting me some time. I promise, we'll talk.'

He was right. No matter what happened they had to at least be able to talk about Holly together, no matter what he made her feel. 'I'm not sure,' she said slowly, loath to admit he was right.

'Scared?' he teased, standing up and holding the car door wide.

She glared at the man. She wasn't twenty and impressionable any more. She wasn't going to fall into his arms at the drop of a hat. They had a child, they had a history and they had a whole heap of issues to resolve.

She was terrified.

CHAPTER NINETEEN

'I CAN'T do this, Nick.'

Nick held the car door, trying to keep cool and sound unaffected, his eyes glued to the glorious amount of leg the split in her dress was affording him—smooth, tanned and oh-so-tempting.

He rubbed his jaw, smothering the rise of heat in his loins. Hell, they *needed* to talk. 'I'm just asking you to come up and talk like two sensible, sane human beings,' he said, surprising himself with the calm in his voice when every part of him was screaming for her.

She glared up at him. 'You're an arrogant, selfish womaniser.'

He raised an eyebrow, feeling a rush of warmth in his chest. 'You have a problem with all the women I've gone out with?' Was she jealous? He hoped so.

'No. Yes. I—' She bit her lip. 'Well, it's not like you've been looking for true love.'

He shrugged. 'That's how men look.' Did she really care what he'd been up to? For her sake or Holly's?

She shook her head. 'Please.'

He knew what she was saying, what she was asking of him, but he couldn't bring himself to concede just yet. 'I don't get this. You're the one that dumped me and ran off to have my baby all by yourself.'

She lifted her chin. 'I did.'

His gut contracted at her defensive tone. Okay. So it was time to stop taunting her. 'I'm just asking for some quiet time with you to resolve this. I promise I won't do anything that you don't want me to.'

She stared at him, letting her gaze drop slowly to his blue tie, down to his trouser belt, down to his shoes and up again. 'You promise?'

He gripped the car door tightly. 'I promise to be a complete gentleman. I just didn't want to be some-where with noise and interruptions. I promise.' He crossed his chest with his fingers. As long as she didn't look at him like that again. Damn.

She slid out of his car and stood up, straightening her dress over her curves. 'You weren't a boy scout,' she stated, shooting him a narrowed look.

He swallowed hard, trying to keep his gaze on her face and not on the hand running over her hips. 'I know, but it looks sincere.'

'Great.' She sauntered towards the front entrance of his building, her hips swaying provocatively. 'Just great.'

Nick followed. Cripes, he wished he were. How was he going to survive being with her, wanting her, aching for her, with her right in front of him, in his place, talking about his baby, their baby?

Hell, he wasn't a saint.

Nick closed the door firmly behind her.

Skye felt the thud ripple through her. What on earth was she doing? Was she insane? She didn't have enough will-power to resist Nick Coburn. Her fingers tensed and she dropped one end of her wrap.

Nick caught it and slipped the wrap off her shoulders, flinging it over a hook on the wall where coats hung. 'So?'

'Nice place,' Skye blurted, striding out of the close entry and into the sitting area, feigning an interest in the furniture and the room, anything rather than look Nick in the face.

'Thanks. Lisa did it for me. She has a real flair.'

She moved around the room, running her fingers along his timber shelves, filled with books. His sister had done a good job. 'Been here long?'

'A year or so, but I'm thinking I want to move on. You know, a house in the suburbs with a big back yard.'

'Oh?' She bit her lip. He couldn't still think that they could be together, as a family, after that blonde…

He sauntered to the kitchen nestled in the far corner of the large open-plan expanse, shrugging his jacket off and tossing it across a bar stool as he passed. 'Would you like a drink?'

She shot him a glare. Was he for real or was he playing out one of his seduction rituals—get her tipsy and into his bed, making mad passionate love to her, all night…?

A light thrill rippled through her, and she looked towards his windows and the view of the city from them.

'Tea, coffee?' he asked, filling the kettle and snapping it on.

She let out the breath she'd been holding. Stupid fantasy. Of course he didn't want to seduce her—they needed to talk. 'Tea, I guess, please.'

Nick opened a cupboard, pulling at his tie. 'I have hot chocolate if you'd prefer.'

Her body warmed. 'Please.' How could it be fair that he still remembered the little things about her when he was so hopeless when it came to commitment?

He deftly plucked two cups from the cup tree and slid the sugar bowl over to where the cups sat.

She moved closer, slipping on to a bar stool, her heart thundering against her chest. 'So?'

He leant on the bench, facing her. 'So, Holly is my daughter. And you knew you were pregnant with her when you decided to leave me. So why do it?'

She dragged in a ragged breath. 'Because I would have ruined your life.' And still would.

'No.' He shook his head. 'Losing you nearly ruined my life.'

She stared across the kitchen to the stainless steel pots hanging above the stove. 'You're just saying that.'

Nick sighed. 'Holly is a beautiful little girl, Skye. You did an amazing job raising her on your own.'

She shrugged. 'I had my family.'

'I know. But you could've had me too,' he said gently.

She shook her head, raising her eyes to meet his brilliant blue ones. 'I couldn't let you sacrifice everything you'd worked for.'

He shook his head. 'I was a fool. I didn't know what *I* wanted.'

She chewed her bottom lip, running her hand along the smooth, rounded edge of the bench. 'What are you saying?'

He reached over and took her hands in his. 'I'm saying I want you both in my life.'

'Really, Nick?' she breathed. Could she take the chance that he was being honest and above board and wasn't just *doing the right thing*? 'You didn't want a child then, last week or yesterday. What makes you think I'd believe you want one now?'

'Because I'm here in front of you, telling you that I want you and Holly in my otherwise boring and mundane life.'

She moistened her lips. She couldn't believe him, not when her little girl's future was at stake, no matter what he made her feel. 'Despite the fact that your father would totally have a fit over another son getting caught up with a family?'

'Yes.'

She swallowed hard. 'Despite the fact that we could severely cramp your career goals if you decided to spend time with us rather than on furthering your career?'

'Yes.'

She stared at him. He was saying all the right things…but she couldn't let herself fall for it. Giving in to Nick now was no guarantee he was going to stick around and be there for Holly. She stiffened. And there was no way in hell she'd have her daughter experience the pain of being discarded and left behind that she had had as a child.

'Despite the fact that until now you didn't want a family of your own?' she bit out, the words like bile on her tongue.

'Yes.'

'Well,' she murmured, stalling. She knew he could twist and use words to his own ends. No matter what…she couldn't bring herself to concede. 'That may be enough for you, but I won't let you make that sacrifice out of duty.'

She lifted her chin. She'd managed okay so far. She could keep going alone no matter how lonely it was not to have someone to share Holly with. She loved him too much for him to lose everything he'd worked for, dreamed of, wanted. And she was sure he'd hate her eventually…for robbing him of his freedom.

Nick shook his head. 'It's not just your choice. She's my daughter too and she deserves a father in her life.'

She sighed. He was so right, but her daughter deserved more than what she had got. 'One who's going to be there for her. Who won't run off with the first leggy blonde that walks past and whisks him off to Europe.'

Nick frowned. 'You can't judge all men by your father.'

She glared at him. 'Why not? You judge all families by yours.'

'Touché.'

She sat still, trying not to focus on the heat of

Nick's hands over hers and the delicious warmth they radiated through her body. 'So?'

He squeezed her hands. 'So I want you and Holly in my life, to hell with the consequences.'

'Nick. You don't—' Her voice broke. How could she make him see that what she'd done, what she did now was in his best interests and hers? It wouldn't do anyone any good, especially Holly, to have him in her life, then not, then maybe, then not, like she'd had to endure with a father who hadn't wanted the baggage of kids.

Nick straightened, pulling his hands back. 'Well, at least tell me you're not considering John.'

Skye met his gaze, lifting her chin and throwing back her shoulders. 'There's nothing wrong with him.'

He rubbed his jaw. 'You drive me crazy.'

'Likewise.'

Nick turned to the drinks. He tipped the hot water into the cups, splashing milk in and heaping in the sugar. 'We have a lot to discuss, when you think about it. Is our daughter enrolled anywhere in particular for school?'

Skye's body warmed. Our daughter. It felt so good to hear those words, to hear him acknowledge her, and felt so good that he'd decided to change the subject. 'She's three.'

'You have to get in early at the good schools.'

She took the cup of steaming hot chocolate from him and took a sip. 'Which school did you have in mind?'

He picked up his coffee and took a sip. 'A private

school on the north shore. I've heard the women in the office natter about it a fair bit. It's one of the best.' Nick walked around the bench, slipping on to the bar stool next to hers, looking ahead of him, holding his cup of coffee in his hands.

Skye bit her bottom lip. 'That could mean a lot of travelling for her.'

'We could move closer.'

'We?'

'We. Us. Together.' He put down his coffee on the bench and swung to face her.

'I can't let you do that.'

'I want to.' Nick took her drink from her and drew closer to her, turning her to face him with the lightest touch on her bare shoulder. He cupped her face in his large warm hands. 'I can't imagine missing out on another minute of Holly's life. Or yours.'

'You can't mean that. I know you. I know what you're like with your dogged determination to get to the top.'

'Sure. I want to,' he said softly. 'But the last few years have taught me how lonely it can be.'

Skye chewed her bottom lip. 'You've been lonely, with all those models?'

'Yes. Surrounded by people, by models, by my family, I've been lonely. For you.'

Tears stung her eyes. 'Nick.'

'I can't go back and change the past…no matter how much I'd like to erase some of my ramblings on marriage and children. But I can change the here and now.'

She shook her head, her throat burning. 'Please, Nick, don't. I can't let your father—'

He put his thumb over her lips. 'This isn't about my father. It's about you and me.' He traced the line of her mouth, his gaze intent.

'And our daughter…?' Skye whispered, her chest tight. 'What part does she play? If I didn't have Holly, would we be here, talking now?'

'We wouldn't be talking.' A smile tugged the corners of his mouth, his thumb running along her bottom lip.

A hot ache grew in the pit of her stomach. 'Would you be here, talking to me about commitment and living together and having a life together if I hadn't had your baby?' She bit her lip. Or would he be out with another blonde bombshell?

'Skye.' He stroked her cheeks with his thumbs, his palms cupping her face tenderly. 'We would be here. Of course we would. From the moment I first saw you again I wanted you.'

'That's lust, not love.' She stared into his blue-blue eyes. 'You said you wanted an affair with me, a no-strings affair, not a lasting relationship, not a commitment, not this…what you're proposing.'

'I was an idiot, thinking the last thing you wanted was to be tied down to me,' he said, his voice deep and velvet-soft. 'Look, we can be friends, living in the same house, raising Holly, if you feel more comfortable with that. If you don't like me enough to—'

She shook her head. Not like him? 'I don't think so.'

Nick's hands dropped from her face, his mouth pulled thin. 'I understand.'

'No, you don't.' Skye reached forward, running her hand down his strong jaw and over his mouth, willing to throw caution to the wind one more time for the dream that she'd harboured for four long years. 'I want to be more than friends.'

He opened his mouth, staring at her.

'Far more.' She leant forward and touched her lips to his. If he was willing to take the chance, she could too...and if he was over blondes and work, then where was the problem?

This was what she wanted. His lips against hers, being with him, holding him, keeping him.

'We said we were going to talk,' he murmured, his voice husky, pulling away from her a little.

'Later,' she whispered, standing up and moving closer to him, wrapping her hands around his neck and claiming his mouth.

Nick's arms slipped around her waist, pulling her close, his kisses trailing down her neck, pressing his lips against her bare skin and up again to take her lips.

His large hands slid up along her curves, over her hips and up, cupping her breasts.

'Skye.' His deep voice simmered with barely checked passion.

She ran her fingers through his hair. 'Nick.'

He caught her nipple between his thumb and fingers, and bolts of desire shot through her.

She opened her mouth to him. Yes. It had been too long since she'd been with him. Every inch of her yearned for this, for the experience burned in her brain, four years old.

'Are you sure?' Nick asked, his breath ragged.

She nodded. 'Totally.' More than anything. She couldn't get it wrong this time, not when he wanted them, wanted her in his life, was lonely with models and his career. 'Yes. Oh, yes.'

Nick's hands slid over her butt, pulling her up against him as he stood up. He felt good. She wrapped a leg around him, running her hand through his hair, kicking off her shoes.

'I don't believe this is happening,' he whispered against her ear, kissing her lobe, his breath hot and heavy.

Skye pulled his shirt out from his trousers, slipping her hands underneath, against his hot, hard muscles. 'Believe it.' She felt the swell of excitement in her chest. Dreams really did come true.

Nick lifted her into his arms and strode to his large bedroom, lowering her gently to the ground beside the large bed, sliding her against his hard body as he caught her zip and met her gaze, his eyes blazing with passion.

'Maybe we shouldn't,' he whispered.

A touch of sanity drifted to her, but she pushed it away. She wanted this. Needed this. Nothing was going to stop her. 'We more than should.' She hooked her hands behind his neck and pulled him down to her lips.

He ran his hand down her back, taking the zip with it. He brushed his lips against hers, then pulled back, slowly hooking her straps in each thumb and pushing them off her shoulders. The dress fell to the ground.

Nick let out a breath. 'Skye.' His eyes caressed her as they drifted over the swell of her breasts and her black lace bra, over her flat stomach and down to her lace panties and up again. He shook his head. 'It hasn't been long since we met up—'

She stepped closer to him, flicking open the buttons on his shirt and slipping it off his shoulders to reveal his wide, muscled chest. 'It's been forever since we last made love.'

'Skye...' Nick swept her into his arms, crushing his mouth to hers, their lips burning in the fiery possession.

She ran her hands over his back, down his hot flesh, around his waist, undoing his belt and sliding it slowly from his trousers.

Nick pulled back a little, brushing her mouth with gentle kisses, tasting her, savouring her.

He touched her breasts reverently, tracing the line of her black lace bra with his thumb. 'You fed her by—?'

Skye nodded.

'You're an amazing woman.' He slid his hand behind and unclasped the bra, letting it fall.

He cupped her breasts, catching her nipples between his thumb and fingers, plying her breasts, sending cascades of hot and achy need rippling through her.

She ran her hands over his hot flesh, over his strong chest where she'd once laid her head and listened to his dreams.

'Oh, Skye.' He ran his hands down her waist, over her hips and down her thighs and up again, snagging her panties and pushing them down.

The button on his trousers gave easily and she slid the zipper down. He kicked off his trousers and shoes and reduced the distance between them until his hard, hot body was pressed against hers.

His mouth swooped down and captured hers, taking her weight in his arms and lowering her back on to the smooth silk covers of the duvet.

Nick's mouth captured a breast, drawing her nipple into his mouth and flicking it with his tongue, sending her senses wild.

His hand slid up her thigh and ran through her soft curls. 'Oh, Nick. Nick.'

'You're going to respect me in the morning?' he asked, trailing kisses across from one breast to the other, catching the other hardened peak in his mouth.

'I'm going to respect you all damned night,' she whispered, running her hand down his hard body, grasping him, pleasuring him.

Skye's pulse raced, her blood as hot as her body, her senses wild at his touch, his kiss, his large hands exploring her body.

'Hell, Skye. What are you doing to me?' he groaned, moving lower, trailing kisses down her stomach.

'Well—' She grinned, opening her legs for him, as he pressed hot kisses down the inside of her thighs. 'I could tell you, but I think it would be better if we just let it happen...'

His thumb found her first, sliding deep within her

soft curls, stroking her into a frenzy of passion. She twined her hands in his hair. Then his lips were there, drawing, teasing and playing until her breath came short and sharp and ragged.

She shook with the pleasure of him.

'Nick,' she cried, the urgency in her voice all it took.

Nick drew himself up to her, taking her mouth with his as though he was listening for her desire with the intensity of her kiss, with the depth of her kiss, with the fiery passion she returned his kiss with.

He drew back and looked down into her face. 'I'm going to…respect you for ever.'

He slid inside her. Hot and hard and slow. Driving deep. He felt so good. As if he belonged. As if he'd never left…

Tears stung her eyes as her body filled with the tearing pleasure he was invoking, driving her wild, filling her, completing her.

'Nick,' she whispered, touching his cheek with her lips. 'Oh yes…yes. Yes!'

He held her in his arms, his face in the crook of her neck, his breath ragged and hot. Finally, he rolled beside her.

She lay her head against his chest, savouring the feel of his strong arm around her, listening to the pounding of his heart, wondering what he was feeling but too afraid to ask. Did she want to know if he could love her the way he used to, or was this arrangement just convenient, and without love or any hope of it?

She traced her hand across his stomach. She didn't

want to know, not yet. She wanted to enjoy this now, even if it was an illusion.

Nick pushed back a lock of hair from her face, tracing her cheek with his finger. 'Should we talk now?'

'Later,' she said, pressing her lips against his chest, tracing the lines of muscles, and down. 'Much later.'

CHAPTER TWENTY

NICK watched her, a warm glow in his chest. Her beautiful body was in his arms again, stretched out beside him, her features gentle and serene in sleep, her lips full and inviting.

How could he have let her go? He wanted to slap himself in the head. How could he have been such an idiot to jump to erroneous conclusions and lose her?

Because of his damned big mouth and questionable work ideals he'd lost four years of her life, and all of Holly's. There was no way he was going to lose her again.

Nick pushed a wisp of hair from her face, tucking it back. How in hell was he going to convince her to stay? Last night wouldn't have helped. He should have slowly romanced her, not swept her off her feet and into his bed.

'Hmm.' Skye stirred. 'I have to get home.'

'Yes.' He kissed her bare shoulder. To their beautiful child. And he couldn't wait for them to be together, all together, in a home of their own.

Skye sat up, her breasts full and inviting. She slipped out of bed, her beautiful naked body swaying gently as she walked to the *en suite* bathroom, sending a rush of blood to his loins.

She closed the door behind her.

Nick took several deep breaths. This wasn't the

time to make glorifying her body a new religion. This was the time to solidify his position, get some assurances, guarantees. Last night had to mean something.

Skye opened the door, her hair wet, her body glistening with moisture. 'So, am I going to see you later?' she asked casually. 'Or was that it?'

Nick frowned. 'It?'

She picked up her clothes off the floor, keeping her focus averted from him. 'You know "it". All there was to all your interest in me and Holly. You know, just to get me into bed with you.'

His blood cooled. 'You think that?'

She met his gaze. 'I don't know what to think with you. You confuse me. You epitomize the playboy bachelor yet you're talking about playing families with me and Holly.' She shrugged. 'I just thought, since we'd made love you wouldn't want us any more.'

'Hell.' Nick sprung out of bed and strode to her, pulling her into his arms and holding her. 'Not a chance, Skye. Of course I want you. Everything I said was true.' He cringed at the thought of her thinking him to be so shallow and manipulative.

Skye pulled back, her brow creased. 'You want us?'

Nick brushed his lips against hers. 'Of course I do.' He kissed her, deeper, holding her closer against him, his blood heating.

'Do you want to spend time with us today?' she asked softly, running her soft hands up his back.

'I'm going to see my family today,' he murmured, tasting the fresh soapy skin on her shoulder.

'Great.' Skye ran her hands into his hair, and down his chest. 'I'd love to see them too, and Holly.'

His gut tightened. Damn. He'd hoped to have a bit of time to prepare his father for them, not just appear out of nowhere. Especially in the old man's condition.

Skye's towel dropped to the floor.

Nick groaned, running his hands down her body. 'Yes.' He'd work something out. He had to. He had to make it all right. Somehow.

Skye stood in the corner of the garden, savouring a moment of peace from the Coburns. All the Coburns had arrived for Sunday lunch and the chatter and noise was incredible.

The four Coburn sisters, all grown up now, had swooped down on Holly and whisked her away to play in the backyard playground with Robert's kids.

For his father to be so against kids he certainly had the yard decked out for them...probably Nick's mother's doing.

The announcement that Holly was Nick's child had gone down like a ton of bricks. Sure, they'd appeared happy for him, and happy to see her again, but there was a tension between Nick and his father, and everyone could feel it.

Skye couldn't have missed everyone's coy looks in her direction. The tense looks towards their father then to Holly, as though he was going to explode at any moment.

She'd opted to escape from them all and watch the children play with Holly. Her cousins...

There was something special in being a part of

something larger, as though her little broken family of two had exploded into a generation. She sighed. They belonged.

'Don't tell me you're going to throw your life away like your brother did?' Harry Coburn's voice bit out.

Skye turned to find herself beside an open window. Harry's study window. Her belly tightened.

'It's not like that, Dad,' Nick responded.

Harry coughed heavily. 'You're saddling yourself with a woman and her child now, right when you can really do something with your career?'

'The child is mine.'

'Are you sure? How can you know? There are other ways you can deal with this,' Harry snarled, fighting another coughing fit.

Skye wanted to move but her legs refused. The last thing she wanted was to be heard, to be caught, and she didn't want Nick's close relationship with his father to be hurt.

'You're getting upset,' Nick said, the concern evident in his tone.

'Damned straight I am. And for good reason.'

'Dad, you don't understand.' Nick ran a hand through his hair. How was he going to get his father to understand without hurting him? Without making him sicker than he already was?

Nick knew he was all that was left of the Coburn men that could satisfy his father's need to leave a legacy, more than just offspring, and make a mark in the world.

His father's health was terrible. The doctors said he didn't have long...

Nick sighed. He didn't want to upset him. He strode across the room. 'The partners are looking for someone stable and a good way to show them that is to settle down.'

His father leant forward in his chair. 'So you're not giving up on your career?'

'Not a chance.'

'But what about your duties at home…to her and the child?' his father said, covering his mouth and coughing.

Nick shrugged, holding back the enormity of what he was feeling. 'Skye is used to coping on her own. She's coped for four years without me. It's not that I have to be there all the time…playing husband and father.'

'You don't know how glad I am to hear that, son.' His father leant back in his chair. 'I couldn't have what I really wanted—just didn't have the education—but there's no reason on this earth that one of my sons isn't going to get there.'

Nick patted his father on the shoulder. 'I know, Dad.'

Skye sank down on to the grass, her legs giving way beneath her, her chest tight, making it difficult for her to breathe. So that was his game. She'd known deep down he'd had one, she just hadn't known what. She had hoped it was all above board. All as he said it was.

He hadn't said he loved her. She covered her mouth. He'd said he'd be there for her. She clenched her hands by her sides. But his career always came first.

What a fool she was!

She should never have believed him. He'd probably discard them like used socks once he'd gotten his precious promotion. Or worse, he'd be late home every night because he'd rather have the company of tall, lanky blondes to her and Holly.

She had been right to leave him four years ago. She should have stayed gone and not entertained her fantasies. Sure, she was a hopelessly optimistic romantic. Now she had no choice. She had to be a realist.

There were no castles in the air and no happy-ever-afters…there were only hard truths. And she'd had enough to last a lifetime.

'You're quiet.'

Skye stared out of the car window, watching the blur of trees and houses. 'Yes.'

Nick glanced at her. 'Is there a problem?'

Skye turned around and looked at Holly in her booster seat in the back, her head resting to one side, her eyes closed. She had to do this, for both of them, all of them. 'Yes.'

'And what's that?'

'I've been thinking a lot today and…' She took a deep breath. 'And I've decided that moving in with you, having any sort of relationship with you, is out of the question.'

His hands gripped the steering wheel tightly. 'What?'

'You can see Holly every second weekend if you like,' she stated casually, trying to sound calm and sure of herself when every part of her was screaming for her dream to be true.

'Skye.'

'Or whenever,' she blurted. No point in forcing him into that either. 'You may just be too busy.'

Nick turned the car into her street. 'What's this about? I don't understand.'

She waved her hand dismissively. 'I spoke hastily, I acted hastily...' Skye bit her lip. What could she say to him to end this without giving away that she'd heard him and his father, that she knew exactly where he stood and why he wanted them in his life just now? She lifted her chin. 'You're not what I want.'

Nick pulled the car to the kerb in front of her house and turned to face her. 'It didn't feel that way last night.'

She shrugged, heat burning her cheeks. 'I was... interested in your body. That was all. I let lust get to my head and do the thinking for me and it just won't work out in the long run. Besides...'

'Besides what?'

She grasped the door handle. 'I have John.'

He stared at her, his lips pressed tightly together, his hands clenched on the steering wheel. 'And you've decided this *now*?'

'Yes. Woman's prerogative.' She opened the door.

'Like hell.'

She swung the door wide. 'There's no law to say I can't change my mind.'

'We had a verbal agreement.'

'I was acting under the influence.'

'Of what?' he demanded, his knuckles white on the steering wheel.

She shrugged. 'Of sex.'

'Right. So, you're saying you don't want to share a life with me. That I can't live with you and Holly. That you don't want me in your life, save for a few token visits.'

She nodded, not willing to trust her voice when all she wanted was to fall into his arms and hold him one last time, kiss him one last time.

Skye slipped out of the car, opened the back door and lifted Holly into her arms. She stepped back. Nick was right behind her.

He unbuckled the child seat and wrenched it out of his car, his silence more torturous than an argument.

Skye forced herself to move to the front door. She was doing the right thing. He didn't really want them. It didn't matter what he'd said last night—he was trying to do the right thing by her and Holly, that was all, and secure his promotion.

Her throat burned. She knew that it couldn't last. She couldn't live a lie.

She fumbled for her keys in her bag at the front door, looking up into his handsome face, the confusion burning in his eyes. 'Nick—'

He dropped the seat beside the door. 'No. Don't. I get it. Don't worry. I get it. I don't live up to your ideal husband and father image that you've been concocting in your head from the day your father left you.'

Her chest tightened. 'That's not fair.'

'Tell me about it.' He leant over towards her. 'Goodbye, Skye.' He kissed Holly on the top of her head. 'Have a nice life.'

And Nick Coburn turned on his heel and left.

CHAPTER TWENTY-ONE

SKYE put Holly gently into her bed, her heart aching for what could have been, her eyes stinging with the cruelty of fate.

She pulled her daughter's shoes off. Was he right? Had she created the image of a perfect father after her own had left and she wasn't going to settle for anything less for her child?

Tears ran unchecked down her cheeks. Probably.

Her father had walked out of her life without so much as a goodbye. No presents, no cards, no contact. She'd needed the perfect father then, any father, and she'd had none.

Was she cursing Holly to the same fate? No father, because she couldn't see Nick living up to the image she'd created. Would any relationship with him be better than nothing, for Holly?

The phone rang. The answering machine took the call.

'Skye. It's Nick. I'm sorry. You're right. I've acted like a playboy for so long I should wonder that you even considered me worthy of being anywhere near you or Holly. I just…I wanted to say that if you need anything… Anything at all. Any time. I'm here… And I'll send you some money each week—call it whatever you like, but I'm going to. And I'd like to send our daughter presents. On her birthday. And see

her. See you both, every now and then, if you don't
mind.'

Skye covered her mouth as the warning beep
sounded.

'Give me a call when you're ready…whenever.'
And he hung up.

Her knees gave out beneath her and she sagged to
the floor, covering the sobs rising up her throat.

The church looked good for the Harrison-Brown rehearsal even though there were no flowers adorning
the benches, no decorations around the altar, no lavish
gowns, or tuxes or crowds.

Skye had made a point of appearing extremely busy
for the last half hour since she arrived so she didn't
have to think about talking to Nick until she knew for
sure what she was going to do.

Miss Cynthia Brown stood as though she wore her
wedding gown, her shoulders pulled back, a soft smile
on her face as she looked at her fiancé, Paul, her eyes
shining as though she was Cinderella at the ball.

Skye crossed her arms and watched the rehearsal,
her eyes burning at the magic of making someone
else's dreams come true.

When would be her turn?

Her eyes drifted to the two suited men beside the
bride-to-be. One with eyes only for Cynthia, the other
taller one with eyes for no one.

The blonde bridesmaid, who had dragged Nick off
the other day, wasn't at all pleased by his cool manner
towards her, despite all her efforts. Huh!

Skye crossed her arms over her chest. She wanted

to plan her own wedding. Have her own gorgeous gown. Have Holly dressed up in pink with a basket of flowers. Have a man in her life who loved her.

Why couldn't she help herself?

'You may kiss the bride,' the minister announced with grand aplomb.

Cynthia and Paul kissed, and turned to her.

'Okay, that was great. I have no doubt that Saturday will be perfect.' Skye strode forward. 'Does anyone have any concerns?'

The wedding party shook their heads, looking at each other and smiling as though they were happy in their part in the fairytale wedding.

Skye couldn't help but look at Nick, her chest tight. His manner was aloof, his gaze cool, as though he wanted to melt into the background.

'Okay. Then I'll see you all bright and early Saturday morning,' Skye said, plastering a smile on her face. She was a damned good wedding planner…and dammit, she *could* help herself live her dream!

The group moved off.

Skye stepped forward. 'Mr Coburn, could I have a word with you?' She crossed her fingers behind her back and took a deep breath, trying to slow her racing pulse.

He turned, his blue eyes dull, looking at her as though she was a stranger, as though he'd built a wall between himself and the world.

Skye waited until the rest of the party had left, leaning back against one of the pews, counting the pounding of her heart against her ribs.

Nick shoved his hands into his trouser pockets. 'If this is about Paul's bachelor party, don't worry. I'll look after him and make sure he gets to the church in time.'

She sucked in a deep breath. 'Great. But that's not what I wanted to talk to you about.'

He raised an eyebrow. 'Really?'

She crossed her arms over her chest. 'I wanted to tell you, you were right.'

He looked at her, his blue eyes probing her dark eyes with an intensity fit for intimidating witnesses.

She shrugged, dropping her hands by her sides. 'I have had this idealised version of my father in my mind for years. I thought I knew what I wanted for my baby, but now I'm not so sure.'

Nick shifted his weight on his feet. 'What are you saying, Skye?'

'I'm saying that I'd like you to be a part of Holly's life. You are her father and, no matter who you are or how you live your life, that won't change.'

'What do you mean?'

She shrugged. 'I mean, with how important your career is to you and all, whatever time you can find to spare with Holly will be fine—I won't stand in your way. That's if you want to.'

Nick nodded, his gaze intense. 'Want to? Of course I want to. Nothing is more important to me.'

Skye looked at his shiny black shoes. 'Except your career.'

Nick took a step forward, grabbing her shoulders. 'No. Not my career. Not anything.'

'But you said that Holly and I were a good way to

show the senior partners at your office that you'd settled down—and I don't mind if you portray us that way. If you feel you need to.'

'What?' Realisation dawned on his face. 'Skye—' He ran a hand through his hair. 'You heard what I said to my father?'

'Yes.' She nodded. 'But that's okay. It's all true. I am used to coping on my own and I have no problem now with you playing daddy to Holly whenever you can. That's okay. I'm fine with that.'

'Skye. I didn't mean that stuff. I said it because I couldn't bear to see my father upset. He's so sick and the last thing I want to do is cause him more pain. We'd just dropped a three-year-old child on him... I figured he needed more time—'

'You didn't mean it?' She looked up into his face, pressing her back against the seat.

'No.' He looked stricken. 'Sure, that promotion is important to me but not more important than you and Holly are to me. Hell, Skye. We're talking about our daughter and our relationship here, not a pay packet.'

Skye waved a hand dismissively. 'Okay. Right. It doesn't matter. It doesn't make a difference.'

He lifted her chin with a finger. 'It doesn't make a difference to *us*?'

She shook her head. 'There is no us.'

'There was the other night,' Nick said softly, his voice deep and smooth. 'And you were all for getting a house in the suburbs with me.'

'That was before—'

'Before what?' Nick shook his head. 'Before I said it wasn't true.'

She bit her bottom lip, holding back the tears.
'How can I believe you?'

'Believe in yourself and what you feel for once in
your life, Skye.' And he pulled her into his arms and
captured her mouth, kissing her, making her lips burn
for him. 'I'm not going anywhere,' he whispered,
pulling back. 'You can push me away all you like but
I'm not going to give up on you, on us.'

Her heart fluttered. 'You said on the phone that
you—'

'I lied. I figured you'd be more comfortable with a
relationship on those grounds.'

She couldn't help but smile as the tears bit her eyes.
'You were right.'

'I know.' Nick held her tightly. 'It seemed as
though you were all out for a repeat of four years
ago, shoving me away. But this time I wasn't about
to let you go. I could say I'm sorry for not coming
after you the first time, but I don't think sorry could
ever be enough.'

'Nick.'

He pulled her back and looked into her face, his
blue eyes glowing. 'I'm not going to hurt you, Skye.
I love you.'

He loved her! The words reverberated through her
body and mind like an earthquake, shattering the last
four lonely, sad years into tiny pieces.

'I want you in my life, both of you. I want us to
be a family.'

She bit her lip. Could she risk it? Was love
enough? It hadn't been for her parents... 'I don't

know—can you guarantee me that you won't run off with some leggy blonde—?'

He held her firmly by the shoulders. 'Hell, Skye. Why would I want to if I have you in my life?'

Her belly fluttered. 'Can you guarantee—?'

'Skye, there are no guarantees,' Nick said softly. 'But if you can learn to love me, in some small way we've got as much chance at happiness as anyone else.'

She swallowed the lump in her throat. 'I do love you, Nick. I've always loved you.'

'You did?' Nick's mouth curved into a smile, his eyes deep and blue and bright. 'Then how could you leave me?'

'Because I loved you too much to wreck your life.'

He ran a hand down her cheek and across her lips. 'Well, I love you too much to wreck yours. So you'd better say you'll have me or you'll have an irate lawyer on your hands.'

She took a deep breath, her chest filled with warmth. 'I want you.'

'Then we have everything we need.'

Skye brushed her lips over his. 'Would you be interested…in more children…some time?'

'Absolutely.' Nick beamed down at her. 'I figure I missed out a lot already. I don't intend to miss out again.'

And he pulled her into the warmth of his arms, sealing their love with a kiss, making her dreams come true.

Harlequin Romance®

presents
an exciting new duet by
international bestselling author
Lucy Gordon

Where there's a will, there's a wedding!

Rinaldo and Gino Farnese are wealthy, proud,
passionate brothers who live in the heart of
Tuscany, Italy. Their late father's will brings
one surprise that ultimately leads to two more—
a bride for each of them!

Don't miss book 2:

Gino's Arranged Bride, #3807
On-sale August!

Available wherever Harlequin books are sold.

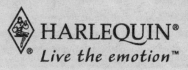

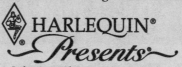
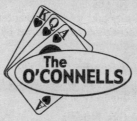
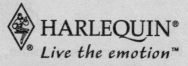

If you enjoyed what you just read,
then we've got an offer you can't resist!

Take 2 bestselling love stories FREE!

Plus get a FREE surprise gift!

The world's bestselling romance series.

HARLEQUIN®
Presents~

Seduction and Passion Guaranteed!

Mama Mia!

They're tall, dark...and ready to marry!

Don't delay, order the next story in
this great new miniseries...pronto!

Coming in August:

THE ITALIAN'S MARRIAGE BARGAIN
by Carol Marinelli
#2413

And don't miss:

THE ITALIAN'S SUITABLE WIFE
by Lucy Monroe
October #2425

HIS CONVENIENT WIFE
by Diana Hamilton
November #2431

**Pick up a Harlequin Presents® novel and you will
enter a world of spine-tingling passion and
provocative, tantalizing romance!**

Available wherever Harlequin books are sold.

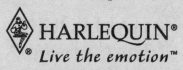

HARLEQUIN®
Live the emotion™

www.eHarlequin.com

HPITALH2

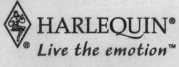